James McComb was born in Scotland, raised in England and America and currently lives in Wales. Works in preparation include *External, The Life and Times of James McComb* and *The Spiritualist.*

# TRUTH AND LIES

# TRUTH AND LIES

## James McComb

Kestrel Books and Gallery
2017

Kestrel Books and Gallery
2 Garth Felin, Brook Street
Hay on Wye HR3 5BQ
www.hay-kestrel.com

First published 2017

ISBN 978 1 874122 37 1

Typeset by RunesAndLetters.com
Printed and bound by ScandinavianBook

# Contents

For those who left early and
those who stayed behind

# The Prostitute's Child

I stopped on the hard shoulder of the motorway coming into London and took a child. Its mother had left it or abandoned it.

I called her 'She-who-waits'.

I took her home and fed her. Days later I left her (she called me Papa by then) to visit a girl of the streets. I met her (her name was Julie or Julia, I forget which) in Soho and together we walked to some flats behind Cambridge Circus. She was the first girl of the streets I had ever visited. She told me her name. I told her mine. I said without thinking,

'I live with the woman I love.'

She smiled and asked me if I had ever picked up a girl such as her before. I said, 'Yes, once, when I was poor and starving. I picked up a girl with long red hair outside a club. She took me up to her room above the club and I gave her all the money I had (which was not very much). In the room, lying in a basket, was an alsation. The girl went to have a bath and came back wearing only a towel, knotted around her breasts. She sat on the bed beside me still wet from the bath and took off her wig.

' "Do you mind?" she said. She had short cropped ginger hair, much less attractive than the wig.'

'Do you not love me anymore?'

I smiled. 'She must have liked me because she let me stay the night. I still remember the smell and feel of her warm, damp body, the feel of my damp prick ejaculating into her, then sleeping in her arms. I woke at dawn and she was sleeping beside me.'

'Then I left.'

'And did you love her?'

'I have never loved any woman.'
We walked in silence.

The girl of the streets said, 'I also live with the woman I love.'
We went into the flats where she lived, or brought clients to, and took the lift. We entered her flat. She took off her dress. I took off my clothes and lay down on the bed beside her. I began to kiss her breasts. 'We're not supposed to be making love,' she said.

She was thin and pretty and, I suppose, while I was with her I did love her. She was cool, almost cold, but I could see that her sapphism was a front. Yes, perhaps she lived with her girlfriend and was cold to me but I could see it would be possible to please her. I said,
'I took a child.'
'You took a child?'
'Yes. She's in my flat.'
'You took a child?' she repeated.

We walked out of her flat together, went down in the lift and back into the street. We walked together towards Soho. It was raining and Julie or Julia opened a thin, green umbrella.
Our steps in pace, she said,
'Where's the mother?'
'What?'
'The child's mother?'
'It has no mother.'
We walked on in silence. Then she said,
'I'm going back to work now.'
'Can I see you again?'
'If you like.'
I went back to my flat and attended to the child, then sat in the cold kitchen and ate a tuna fish sandwich. I have always liked tuna fish, cold or hot, with or without salad. I thought of Julie, her sapphism, of how I needed someone in my life. Perhaps her. I knew I could not keep the child.

We stood in the field in the rain stacking empty boxes in the rubbish dump. The wind gusted the rain into our faces. The boxes were wet through, collapsed and useless. Beside us the baby howled.

I came to a river and tried to jump over but instead I landed in the middle. My feet were caught in the tangle of weeds and branches on the riverbed and I was dragged under.

I heard the baby crying (through dreams of Julie/Julia) and fetched her some milk. I knew, such was the impasse of my life, that I could only be justified in the act of murder.

I sought her out again, waiting night after night in the cold, damp, garish streets. At last I saw her. I followed her, walking quickly, until I was level with her. I turned and looked into her face.
    'Hello Julie.'
    'O, you again.'
    'How are you?'
    'I'm fine. Do you want to see me?'
    My heart was in my throat.
    We walked beneath an arch and along a narrow street until we came to the edge of Soho. We crossed the road towards her flat.
    'How's your child?'
    'I have no child,' I said smiling. 'I just made that up.'
    'O.'
    'How's your girlfriend?'
    'We split up. She was unfaithful.'
    'Unfaithful?'
    'She kept bringing other girls back to the flat. I threw her out.'
    We walked on.
    'So now we're both alone.'
    'You could say.'
    We went into the flats and up in the lift. The lift stopped and the doors opened. We walked along the passage until we came to her flat.

9

She sat on the bed and arched her arms behind her back to take off her bra. She had small, rather pointed breasts; the breasts, I thought, of a lesbian. They were firm, unsucked, unsuckling. I took off my clothes and sat down on the bed beside her.

You don't have a child, I thought.

'I have waited for you all my life,' I said. 'You and I to be here, in this way. Alone.'

I put down my mouth and began to suck her breasts. She put her cold hand in my crotch. After a while I felt my sex stirring.

I kissed her.

'But you don't love me?' she said.

'No.'

We made love on the bed. When I had finished I rolled off her. She lay cold and still, her eyes unmoving.

Three days later, driven by an impulse I did not understand, I returned to the corner where I'd met her. Another woman of the streets approached me. She was dishevelled, with untended hair that may once have been red. Her clothes were rags.

'Would you like to see me?' she said.

'Yes.'

We walked together towards a flat she knew.

'I took a child,' I said.

'I once had a child.'

'Was it called Anne?'

'No,' she said. She laughed suddenly. 'Julie. I left her beside the road, dressed in swaddling clothes, for someone to find. Someone like you perhaps. Did you find her?'

# Dick Francis

The closest friend of my boyhood was Dick Francis. Dick had soft curly hair and an easy, friendly manner; together we propelled ourselves on cushions around the vast living room of his father's house, or cycled like demons up and down his long garden. Our house was big but not as big as his and the size of his garden put ours to shame.

Cubit, Dick's mother, brought us little sponge cakes with sugar on one side and garibaldi biscuits but otherwise left Dick and I to ourselves – the house was big enough for our antics not to disturb her intense studies. She was an architect and liked to draw up plans for buildings and other structures. She sat at her desk with her pince-nez perched on her nose studying her plans and drawings, making the occasional careful amendment, whilst Dick and I imagined ourselves great conquerors or explorers or conducted our mock battles which he would always win.

'Which will you be, Colonel von Hausschmidt or Dick Devil, secret agent?' No matter which I chose I would always lose. Even stout Cortez might fail to locate the Americas, even Herr Hausschmidt might get the better of Dick Devil, as we scooted about on cushions and scoffed our fairy cakes or ran through the house with peals of laughter.

Dick Francis had no brothers or sisters and neither did I. This was a cause of regret, to him especially, marooned as he was in the great house of his father. I was welcome anytime, he told me, putting his arm round my shoulders and grinning.

'But only because I always lose.'

'You'll win one day,' he said.

'Come on. Let's explore.'

We went out into the vast garden. In the garden, beside Dick Francis's father's house, was another house, even larger than his, which had stood empty for many years.

'Have you ever been inside?' I asked him.

'Yes,' he boasted, but I could tell he was lying.

'When?'

'O, often. Come on.'

'No, no,' I said. 'Tell me. Have you ever been inside?'

'Yes,' he replied again. 'I've told you once, how many more times? Come on.'

'No,' I said.

I hung back. Dick wanted to run free as the wind from one end of the garden to the other but I wanted to know what went on inside the great empty house. The house that, for all I knew, was inhabited by spooks or was merely a figment of his mother's mind.

He sulked then, lowering his head and dropping his drooping arm onto my shoulder. I was two years younger than Dick which was perhaps why I always lost. Two years younger and several inches smaller. A mere child. But I had a fertile, furtive imagination. I could easily imagine the interior of the big house. Vast empty rooms, our heels clicking eerily upon the wooden floors; birds' nests in the chimneys. The sudden slam of a door, a clamour of voices, then silence. Pushing open each door upon each empty room, each room holding its breath before our child-like gaze. Then laughing uproariously, or weeping pitifully, at our departure.

'Come,' I said, 'let's explore.'

'Why? I told you,' said Dick. 'I've been inside. There's nothing there.'

'Well, there must be something. Some trace of past occupancy. An old filing cabinet, some discarded papers, a sofa with the stuffing spilling out...'

'No,' said Dick, 'nothing, nothing at all. The house is empty.'

'There's emptiness and emptiness,' I said, peevishly. 'Anyhow, I'd like to see for myself.'

'No.' He was insistent now. 'We cannot.'

'Why not?'

'I am forbidden.'

'Well, even so,' I said, 'I can. Here, see.' There was a half open window above our heads and before he could stop me I'd shinned up a drain pipe, pushed up the window and dropped to the floor inside.

The room was vast and dark. I could hear Dick uttering childish cries but I ignored them. After all, he was as capable of shinning up a drainpipe as I. Now was not the time for childish things, for games of fantasy, but for uncovering the real world and our places in it. I crept stealthily across the vast room to a double door that hung ajar and led, I assumed, to the interior of the house. I heard the fluttering of a trapped bird behind the crumbling plaster; a broken statue of Venus de Milo lay toppled and tilted on the floor. Rooms were full of scattered papers, old sofas, typewriters cut off in mid key, exactly as I'd imagined them. A plate of cakes remained upon a desk just like the plates Dick's mother would bring us when she tired of her studies. A lipstick-smudged photograph fluttered to the floor beneath my feet. I heard, or thought I heard, the click of footsteps coming from the rooms above. And then, most surprising of all, voices.

Is this place inhabited? I wondered.

I made my way softly upstairs not wishing to be seen. I followed the voices but the voices remained one step ahead of me. The rooms, though full of clutter, seemed uninhabited. A half-drunk cup of tea, a wall calendar, an epiphany chart. A burst of laughter from a neighbouring room was followed by a burst of light, as though the Angel Gabriel had descended among us.

'Goodness, who's this?' said a voice. I turned to see a man with whiskers standing beside me. 'What have we here, what indeed? A young snipe?' He seemed amiable and harmless enough; I let him pick me up and swing me round before gently replacing me on the floor. 'What's your name?' he asked, and I invented a name for myself – Michael. 'Michael,' he said, 'Michael and his host of angels. Do you have a host of angels?' 'No,' I said. He stooped down and looked into my eyes quite seriously. 'Now tell me,' he said, 'where are you from? Who sent you?'

# Darkstar

They are on a perfectly normal road at first. Then, quite suddenly, the huge car veers left and they vanish into a density of mirrored green. Foliage dwarfs a long close-boarded wooden fence high upon a bank, like a barrier between two worlds.

They descend: a road without end.

The driver, Percy, coughing continuously, applies his thumb to the horn. The visitor jumps and bangs his head against the roof of the car. The horn blares, overwhelming even the racket of Percy's cough. The visitor sits up straight in his long grey coat, half-deafened.

Unceasing, they blister down into the mirrored green. Round a sharp, steep bend. Ascend.

'Are we nearly there?' he says.

The driver does not reply. Perhaps he is deaf, deafened by his own terminal racket.

They climb steadily towards the light. The visitor glimpses large, ancient houses set back at intervals from the road amidst oak, plum and cherry trees. They progress past these houses in perfect silence, a silence broken only and irregularly by the racket of the driver's terrible cough.

The man is dying, he thinks.

'This is Lucy,' says Canteloupe. 'The maid.'

She is a comely maid: eighteen or nineteen years, he judges, with raven-dark hair and mischievous blue eyes.

A bell has been rung and replaced upon an antique marquetry chest. The walls of the hallway are lined with oak; to the left, beyond what appears to be a cloakroom, a staircase leads to the

15

floors above. The walls are covered with Spy cartoons featuring public figures from a distant time – Disraeli, Gladstone, Curzon, Rosebery, Shaftesbury. In the corner, below the stairs, there is a stand containing sticks.

His eye alights upon one of the sticks, a stick with a pearl handle encrusted with gold and what appear to be diamonds.

Lucy stands gazing at him, her hand held out for his coat.

'You are wearing a coat, man.'

'What… O, I am sorry, Canteloupe.'

'Why?'

'I am sorry that I have not properly explained myself. Let me see. Where I come from – I come from the town, as you know – anyway – where I come from it is cold. It is necessary, therefore, to wear a warm garment such as a coat. That is the reason…'

'There is no need for it here.'

'No. No, indeed.'

'Take it off.'

'Yes, Canteloupe.'

Meek as a lamb he begins to remove his coat. Whilst doing so, his eye is drawn back to the pearl-handled stick.

'My,' he says, 'what a handsome stick. May I?'

His coat half on and half off, he reaches forward awkwardly for the stick.

'Leave it be!' she cries, in a voice of thunder.

He jumps back, quick as a chameleon's tongue.

'That is a magic stick.'

'Of course. I am sorry.'

'It belonged to my late husband.'

'Ah – I'm sorry.'

'It belongs now, not to him, but to another.'

'I didn't know…'

'How could you?'

'I'm sorry.'

'It belonged, for example, to my niece. Dead now. Drowned. Like a fish.'

'I'm sorry…'

'Why? It was not your doing. Now, give your coat to Lucy.'

He frees himself from his garment and hands it to the maid. Her hand, intentionally or otherwise, touches his as he does so and her blue eyes settle upon his face. He tries to withdraw his hand but the maid presses her hand to his, fixing their two hands together beneath the coat. He smiles politely and tries to disengage but finds his hand fixed tight and the maid's blue eyes upon his. The maid smiles at him.

Inside the vast chamber Percy limps slowly towards the tack room to sit wearily upon an upturned saddle and smoke a cigarette.

He sees Percy. He sees the polished brasswork and gleaming woodwork of ancient carriages.

From another time, he thinks. A more charitable time, perhaps. Or perhaps not.

A time, anyway, of which he knows nothing.

He imagines the place as it was: small, noisy groups of people making their way from the house to the great chamber to harness, or superintend the harnessing of, horses. To gallop like gladiators through the flat fields of this wide flat land, two abreast, even, he supposes, to fix small broadswords to the axles of the turning wheels to hack off the ankles of any who might be rash enough to stand against them.

Only the horses remain. To his left are the stables, the horses' heads ruminative above the stable doors: a bay with a blazoned stripe; a small chestnut with a golden mane; a black horse, tall and imposing, that rears up and whinnies at the sight of him. Fixes him with its startled eye.

'My husband lost his mind. That of course was later. Mercury. Mercury in the spaghetti.'

The woman and the maid seem to blur before his eyes. He watches one while the other speaks…then turns to address the speaker only to find she has fallen silent.

His gaze returns to the maid. That she is comely there is no doubt. More than comely: prettily freckled, pertly bosomed, the face of an angel. Her blue eyes twinkle as he strives unavailingly to remove his hand from hers. A sudden fear envelopes him – that he will give his coat to the maid and never see either again. That he will fall out with these strangers and need to leave but will be unable to find his coat and will be stuck here for ever.

The woman, Canteloupe, continues to speak as he and the girl struggle soundlessly.

'It was only a matter of time. What difference did it make? Of course, it is not a nice way to go. You have met my neighbour, Darkstar?'

The words swirl around his head like words floating in empty space. He has little idea what the woman is talking about though must assume it is him she addresses. Her husband is, of course, in one respect at least, the reason for his visit…he who vanished from public view forty years earlier and lived out his days, he supposes, here.

'I am sorry, Canteloupe, I did not catch…'

'Darkstar. He owns…' she waves her hand airily '…the land around. You know. The land beyond the mirrored green.'

'O, no. No, I do not think so.'

'But you passed?'

He thinks for moment. What is she talking about? He feels the girl's hand moving against his beneath the coat, to which he is holding fast even as she tries to prise it from his grasp.

'Passed? Ah yes! Yes, indeed. We passed…the fence…the fence that separates…'

'And the mirror? The mirror beside the road?'

'I saw no mirror, Canteloupe.'

'Ah. That is a shame. Without the mirror…'

Her mind drifts momentarily into silence.

'And Percy? Did you see Percy?'

'Percy? O, yes. Yes, of course…Percy. In the tack room.'

'He is an agent from the other side.'

'The other side?'

'The other side, man. Are you unaware of the other side?'

'I…no.'

'He is not like us. He is from there.'

The girl's hand caresses his, quite gently…yet each time he tries to remove his hand he finds it once again locked to hers. He turns to look at her. Her eyes are dark, dark as the moon. He fathoms nothing. She lifts her spare hand to her mouth as if to stifle a giggle.

'Follow me,' says Canteloupe.

'We will start upstairs,' says Canteloupe. 'Then we will go to the cellar.'

She seems older, wearier, now. He follows her up the stairs, past framed paintings of horses and dogs, to the landing. She turns left and shuffles along a long dark corridor.

She has a limp, he notices, one knee not bending quite as it should.

'I cannot imagine why you think these people do not intend us harm.'

'People, Canteloupe?'

'Those who have sent you. Those to whom you belong.'

She stops outside a door. It is so dark he can barely see. She pushes open the door. Some creature flies past his face and flutters into the furthest recesses of the room.

Daylight: lattice windows looking onto a wide plain and distant hills. In the centre of the plain a lake, surrounded by trees.

Everything about the room smells of antiquity and disuse. Heavy wallpaper, unchanged since before the war, an ancient lighting system controlled by pulleys, a water-jug on the commode covered in dust. The only inhabitants, bats.

She turns to face him.

'This will be your room.'

'Thank you, Canteloupe.'

They proceed back along the passage in the same fashion,

Canteloupe limping, he following. I have always followed, he thinks to himself. As a child, I followed my parents. As a young man, I followed any who would lead me. Now, at the end, I follow Canteloupe.

They arrive at the bathroom, the last room on the left, the room before Canteloupe's room. The room no-one, least of all he, may enter.

He dismisses the thought. Tries instead to remember the sequence of events that led him to this place. But he remembers only disparate images...Percy coughing...the car speeding down through the mirrored green...the black horse rearing, hurling globs of phlegm in his direction...

'Well?'

They are standing in the bathroom. There is an ancient iron bath with brass taps and an old-fashioned plug, a long cylinder which may be manoeuvred, like the lights in his room, up or down. A dusty chandelier which hangs crookedly from the ceiling. And beyond the window the same perfect view, ice and silence.

'Charming,' he says.

Canteloupe sighs but does not speak. He sees, beyond, the hills where he rode as a child, the horse flying away with him, like Pegasus.

'My nephews would see me dead. Make no mistake.'

'No, Canteloupe.'

She turns to fix her tired eyes upon him but does not, did not, utter.

He follows her out of the bathroom and back down the stairs. Past portraits of horses and dogs to the hallway. Now she is walking ahead of him through dark passages lit only by candle-light. They are heading through darkness towards more darkness. The only light is the light from the huge red candles that fizz and flicker and die.

They find themselves in a dark hallway. There is, he sees, with a sudden surge of hope, light – a sliver of red light beneath a heavy oaken door. They will, he imagines, go through the door into some inner recess of the house – perhaps, he thinks, with a hope that borders insanity, Canteloupe will spare him. But instead she peers down at the very floor beneath them.

'Here we are, man.'

Canteloupe reaches down and tugs at a rope-handle set in the floor. A trap-door opens and he sees, by an even dimmer light, a light that seems to come from nowhere, a wooden ladder leading down into pitch darkness.

'There are frogs down there. If you listen carefully you can hear them sing.'

He has no wish to descend but knows he has no choice. She is standing there with the trap door open and the rope-handle in her hand.

'Down there, if you listen, you will hear the songs of frogs and the voices of the dead.'

'Thank you,' he says.

He peers down into the darkness, uncertain whether or not to proceed. He could, he thinks, simply walk away, collect his coat and leave. But would it be so simple? First to find his coat. The pretty maid has it no doubt, has no doubt already searched the pockets to see what he has, though of course he has nothing. And, even were he to find his coat, how would he go, back up through the darkness, up through the mirrored green? And, were he to go, who would know him?

'Down,' says Canteloupe. 'Down into the mirrored green.'

He descends, rung after rung.

There will be frogs, he thinks. Shimmying about, jumping in their foamy way upon his broken limbs.

Looking up he sees only the ghostly face of his hostess peering down at him.

'It must be wonderful,' he finds himself saying, 'to live here. So peaceful.'

21

'Nothing wonderful or peaceful about living here.'

'Being away from the crowds, I mean. And the noise.'

'There is no noise, except when particles of light collide.'

He is lying awkwardly, as though upon snakes of coal. His shirt is warm and wet and he knows at once it is soaked in blood. He puts down his hand, tentatively feels through the shirt to the flesh.

He has fallen, like Daedalus. Flown too near some hot-headed angel…incurred, for some reason, the wrath of the gods.

He opens his eyes, closes them. Opens them. At last he finds what he is looking for: a source of light. Dim, distant, faint, an aperture of some sort set high in the roof of the cellar.

# Apotheosis

Start here at the starting point.

I have lost my cat. I am searching high and low. High, because my cat can jump. I have searched on top of the wardrobe and behind the wardrobe. I do not know at this stage whether I am searching for a dead cat or a living one. My search has not yet become a murder enquiry. After all, cats wander.

My cats are often found in the street associating with other cats. Yet they have no need to do this for this house is theirs. A cat came in from the outside in pursuit of one of my cats. I chased it away. Next day it was back, howling at the door. It was a tom-cat, I surmised. My cat, the cat in question, was a feline minx named Henrietta.

Tom and Henrietta.

However, this cat, this Tom, howled outside my door.

I considered various options:

Put up with the howling. Ignore it. Stay calm;

Get rid of Henrietta;

Find a way to deter Tom from his howling.

It seems that, inadvertently, I have effected option two. Got rid of my own cat. I have no memory of this. But that does not mean it hasn't happened. Perhaps I have got rid of my cat without remembering it.

I went out this morning at six a.m. I remember the time because it was unusually early for me. Normally I do not get up till nine or ten. This morning I rose at six. I walked the streets and saw people hurrying to work. At least I assume they were hurrying to work – perhaps they were hurrying from work. No – why would they be hurrying from work at such an hour?

It occurred to me that I could go down to the high street and rob a shop. True, when I rose at six I had no thought of robbing a shop. Besides, what shop would be open? But someone must come in early, I thought, to tidy up or sweep, to stack or take deliveries.

Delivery drivers keep very strange hours. The normal code by which we live means nothing to them. Nothing in their lives is normal. They might set off from a depot at two in the morning and arrive at the shop at six. A four-hour drive through the night. But which day are they in? The previous day, or the day in question? Do they ever sleep?

I imagine they drive for a certain length of time then park and curl up in some sort of bunk behind the cockpit for a certain number of hours then repeat the process, stopping only to fill up the vehicle with goods, or empty it. The days themselves cease to matter.

These drivers have needs that must be catered for.

Food is one. They need food to keep themselves going.

Their mental stimulation is provided by the mathematical intricacies of routes and the often complicated language of road-signs.

They need sex from time to time, also, these drivers, for, despite the strangeness of their lives, they are subject to normal human urges.

The need for food is easily remedied. There are special cafés dotted up and down the concourses these drivers wander. These cafés have particular characteristics. They are rarely cleaned. Burly men in colourless overalls sit leaden-arsed on cheap benches in front of filthy formica-top tables and hungrily slurp huge mugs of coffee into their nicotine-raddled throats.

They are like the children of larks.

Huge fry-ups follow. There are a number of ingredients. Eggs. Sausages (always cheap ones, pasty pink, made from offal and the worst off-cuts). Tomatoes (tinned). Bacon – the thin, tasteless Danish variety. Beans, baked, from a can. Potatoes. White bread.

24

Toasted white bread. And grease, little different from the grease that powers their motors.

The waitresses are middle-aged and worn down by care. Some are married, sometimes to men who stay at home all day. Some are unmarried – unwanted, or too sharp-tongued.

They see the drivers as little boys.

The easiest way to cope, on both sides, is with coarse wit.

The drivers might say:

'Hey, Beryl, bring us a lovely pair of melons!'

or

'Hey, Rita, have a look, there's a sausage on my lap!'

The waitresses either ignore this or respond in kind.

'You want melons? This isn't the Ritz hotel, you know!'

'Call that a sausage? My little boy's got a bigger sausage than that!'

They grapple platonically, these waitresses and truckers, yet it is not, in the end, the waitresses these truckers want.

Two women displaying high levels of cleavage suddenly clip-clop in. They're dressed in short skirts and low tops. Just about everything on show. One is over made-up and overweight but the other, the younger one, is a little beauty.

She's the one for me, or would be.

They sit down, this pair, and ignore the men. Also, for whatever reason, the men ignore them.

Perhaps they are already spoken for.

The young one, the little beauty, orders a strawberry milkshake. When it comes, she puts down her head, sucks in a strawful then lifts the straw and blows milkshake bubbles at her blowsy friend. The bubbles lurch through the air like ill-guided missiles before alighting clingingly upon the blowsy friend's bosoms.

The blowsy one is not amused.

'Here Rita, you silly bitch,' she says. 'Whatya do that for?'

'It's only milk,' says Rita. 'Back where it belongs.'

'You silly cow,' she says, wiping the milk bubbles off her

bosom. 'I ought to put you over my knee and spank you. A spanking's what you need.'

'That'll be the day,' says Rita, blowing another strawful in her friend's direction.

'The day today!' she squeals. She stands up and shakes the milk bubbles off her bosoms in the direction of Rita. Rita lifts her arms in mock surrender. 'Help, help,' she says.

The truckers, bizarrely, ignore this carry on. Engrossed in their fry-ups, studying their red-top newspapers or slurping down their big mugs of tea.

Outside, in the lorry park, other girls are doing the rounds.

One approaches a lorry and taps on the door (the windows on these machines are too high up for tapping on). The lorry driver, who is half asleep, leans down and opens the window.

'What is it?'

'Got a cigarette?'

The lorry driver puts on his glasses and squints down at the girl. She looks okay. Not bad. Quite pretty in her way. She isn't young, maybe early forties, with a gingery tint. Care-worn, as though life has treated her cruelly. But she has an honest face.

He knows what she wants and she knows what he wants.

What he wants is obvious. Sex. He has been on the road for days, weeks, shuttling up and down the black tarmac. Days become nights and nights become days. Sometimes he sleeps in the night, sometimes in the day. His hours are not structured to night and day. He drives for eight hours, sleeps for eight, drives for eight. The days fall out of synch with one another. He has to be at a certain place at a certain time, that is all.

She is turning to go but there is something about her, something, perhaps, that reminds him of his childhood.

'What's your name?'

She stops, turns. Looks up at him.

'Katya.'

'Where are you from, Katya?'
'Poland.'
'Do you need a lift?'
She shrugs. Not exactly. Maybe.
'Do you need a lift, Katya?'
'Really, only a cigarette.'
He takes off his glasses, rubs his eyes. Puts them back on. He sees that she is quite small. Earthbound, a nature goddess, not the long-legged model type. Maybe she is selling sex, maybe just begging. He doesn't know. All he knows is that what she wants is not what he wants, exactly.

'I'll buy you a cup of coffee,' he says. 'And a pack of cigarettes.'
'Okay.'
'Wait,' he says, and disappears.

He leaves the window open. Maybe she will stick around, maybe not. He pulls on his shirt and trousers. It is a warm evening. There are lorries pulling in and out, shunting across the black tarmac, hissing to a stop or bellowing like beasts in the slaughter-house. He knows half the drivers here, by sight anyway. He checks his tacho – he has two more hours. Checks his money. Returns to the window.

She is still there.

He winds up the window and opens the door.

There is a woman lying on the pavement and I almost walk right over her. I see her just in time and stop. She has dark hair and a pretty face. Though she is lying on the pavement, apparently unconscious, her eyes are open. I lean down to address her.

'Are you okay?'
She is looking straight at me. Her eyes are blue.
'Are you okay?'
It seems pointless asking again. A small crowd gathers round.
'She's drunk,' someone says.
'She's had an epileptic fit,' someone else says.
I take her home.

I abandon my plans to rob a shop (there is always tomorrow and, besides, it would have been almost too easy. You wait for the delivery driver to show up, wait till he's arguing the toss with the shopkeeper, then nip inside the back of his lorry and conceal yourself. Open up a few crates, find what you want and out again. These guys never look where they're going. These guys work to a schedule. Even if they caught you they wouldn't have time to do anything about it.)

I prop her up in a corner of the kitchen. She stares at me glassy eyed.

'I've lost my cat.'

'Katherine.'

'Suzy.'

'Pirbrigge Road.'

'Pirbrigge?'

'Second left. Second left and first right. Halfway down on the left. No, sorry, right.'

'It depends where you're coming from.'

'Ireland. Generations of us. They ran out of names for us. I wasn't the only Katherine!'

'The past is still present. Present in the present. All those Katherines…'

'Yes. My great-grandmother was the split image…'

'Of what?'

'I had a lover once. His name was Carl. He was from Africa. Now…' she shrugs '…now…'

'Tell you what,' I say. 'I'm waiting for my woman to come home. She hasn't been home in days. If she doesn't come home today, why don't you and I go out on the town?'

'I'd like that. I'm sorry. I'm epileptic. I had an epileptic fit.'

'Are you epileptic?'

'It's not dangerous. It's not as bad as it looks.'

'Unless you fall under a bus.'

'O ha ha. No, you know when you're going alright.'

'Do you take tablets?'

'I could help you look for her.'

Together we search the house for my cat. My cat is called Suzy. She is a recalcitrant beast. I show my new friend Katherine all Suzy's hiding-places. Behind the cupboard. In the cupboard. On top of the cupboard. Believe me, there's nowhere in this house that cat can go except I'll find her.

'Does she wander?'

'Yes. All cats wander.'

'Except house-cats.'

'Yes, except house-cats.'

When we get to the bedroom Katherine flops down on the bed.

'O,' she says. 'I'm exhausted. Do you mind if I have a little sleep?'

I go downstairs and hunt for food. My partner, with whom I live, is into home-cooking. She's also vegetarian. So what I expect to find, somewhere, is the remains of a home-cooked loaf of bread and some of her strange spreads. Miso, for one. I hate miso but often it's all I get. When the milkman comes – when, that is, I'm up, either because I've risen early or, more likely, because I haven't slept – I buy everything he's got. At least I did, until the money ran out. It isn't great – white bread, thin bacon, battery-hens' eggs, too-creamy milk – but it keeps me going.

My partner, with whom I live, is a demon for cooking up her strange stuff but most often she's absent. She goes without warning or explanation. I can't call her – I don't know where to call. If she's gone back to the subject of her most recent affair, Aloysius the Irish poet, there's no hope at all – being a poet, he doesn't have a phone. He talks crap, like 'If you aren't receiving me already, man, a telephone won't make any difference.' I've warned him off several times but he ignores me, and back to him, unless and until some new fancy crosses her path, she goes. She's been with me (she says) for six months but my memory of this is inexact. Still, as often as not, I wake without her.

Aloysius-the-telephoneless is an ass of the first degree. He possesses only two suits – one velvet and red, the other pure white. He never wears a tie, only a cravat.

'When I met you,' she said, 'you weren't the only can in the pack. You never knew about Archie did you?'

'Who the fuck's Archie?'

'What I will say,' she said, 'is that he plays the trombone.'

All this bizarre talk was doing my head in.

I find some bacon in the fridge, so old it's turned green. I lift it to my nose – strangely, it is odourless. I wonder if it will cook up. I love bacon – my partner, the woman I live with, claims to be vegetarian but I've seen her eating bacon. She's eaten bacon with Aloysius. Her pretence of vegetarianism is no more than that – a faddish, disconcerting pretence. Like the cloaks she wears and the wrap-around shades and the flowers in her hair.

I turn on the grill. Gas comes pouring out but the automatic ignition no longer works and there are no matches. I need to find a light of some sort. There's nothing around. All I can find on the table are rubber bands and pieces of newspaper and empty tins of cat-food. Books too – books with reductive titles like *Being and Nothingness* and *Beyond Good and Evil*. And her stuff: lipstick, hair bands, flowers.

I find a lighter: click click click. Nothing. My theory is that, somewhere inside this demented toy, there must be a spark. Think of history's accidental sparks: the great fire of London, the great fire of Alexandria, the great fire of Rome. This wretched toy could have caused any one of them, despite there being no visible spark, for it carries within itself the possibility of a spark.

I turn the gas taps back on and hold the lighter immediately above the fast-flowing gas. Click click click.

Nothing. Just an outpouring of gas.

You can smell the gas. It has an intoxicating smell. It reminds me of visits to the dentist's chair. My mother outside waiting. I alone in that capacious room. Were my teeth really that bad? Or was it some strange conspiracy? Either way it reflects ill on my mother.

There's nothing wrong with my teeth.
So how come I spent so much time in the dentist's chair, smelling the ethereal gas?

I breathe in the gas. I can feel my head beginning to go. Like a face full of fur-balls, my head expanding. You feel this great mental awakening, as though you could divine the secrets of the universe. Together with a great feeling of peace. Knowing I will wake up as I did then, in the dentist's chair, my mother in her red lipstick and fur-coat talking to the dentist then turning to me with a smile.
 I breathe in the gas. I'm about to pass out when I remember that I've lost my cat.

I go upstairs and look down where she is sleeping. The sun echoes into the room, evaporates upon the still breathing walls.
 She is lying on her back, one arm flung carelessly above her head. Her blue dress has ridden up above her knees revealing the straps of her suspender belt, the clips that attach to her black stockings.
 I need to find a light. And a cigarette. I cannot find either. She has them, presumably, with her.
 I feel no guilt in rummaging through Katherine's bag, the bag that was around her neck when I found her.
 There will be other things too in her bag:
 an address book;
 a used tissue, smeared red;
 contraception (a packet of pills or a packet of condoms);
 her national insurance card or her passport, something anyway with her address;
 a diary, perhaps, with his own name there.

31

# Truth and Lies

Back in the halcyon days, when we lived in one small room called Heaven, I decided one Christmas that I needed to go away to write. I could not put any deadline on this. I had been writing intermittently all year, going to my small study along the passage from our room, writing in longhand in a yellow exercise book, a bar of chocolate and a jar of whisky on the desk before me. Some days I would write a page or two, other days just a few lines. There was no urgency of plot or narrative. I was constructing sentences entirely for their beauty and their philosophical content. Like Dylan's *A Hard Rain's A-Gonna Fall* I thought every line could be a song in itself.

The story I was writing was about an Irish freedom-fighter called Ramon and his sidekick, an effete Englishman known only as Bear. Ramon was based on a young man I'd known, in fact shared a house with, in Dublin two years earlier. He may well have been a freedom-fighter. He was certainly a thief and he never stopped talking except to fart. Then, poised in mid-flow, he would turn and crane his neck over his shoulder. 'Be quiet now with the back-chat' or 'Don't back-chat me' he would instruct his behind. The house itself was freezing cold and we did not share facilities – my room was bedroom, kitchen, dining room and living room all rolled into one. 'Leave the oven on at night,' the young man upon whom I based the character Ramon advised. It did the trick so well that by the end of my time there I was sleeping through the day and not rising till the evening; I would eat my dinner and go out to a pub or club before coming home and writing through the night. It was there that the story of Ramon was born. It wasn't until I returned to England and was contacted by my bank that I

32

discovered that that same young man had, on one of his frequent visits to my room, located and made use of various bits of my chequebook.

Our life in our small room called Heaven had become too easy and at the same time too complicated. We stayed in bed all morning, Sheilagh and I, while children ran riot through the house. At lunchtime I went to the pub and ate chicken sandwiches and drank beer. In the afternoons, with my bar of chocolate and jar of whisky at hand, I constructed my sentences. My work became so spare, so relaxed and unhurried, that in the end I was just choosing a word at a time and juxtaposing it with another entirely for its perceived beauty, for the pictures it created in my head. I made no concession to meaning. I did not realise then that in this I was merely following much greater poets than I – Prynne and his followers, even Beckett himself (though Beckett's work never lacked meaning to me).

In the evenings, exhausted by my labours, I retreated from my study and we sat in our room together, drinking tea, smoking cigarettes and joints and listening to records, or making our own music: scything into the blackness in the timeless moment of our love-making. I wanted her flesh at all hours of the day and night and she wanted mine; to go inside and by going inside to go beyond, to emerge somehow different; to re-arrange the structure of the world.

But the situation was complicated. We didn't live alone. When Sheilagh came, others came in her wake: her son, Alexander, her friend Myla with her two small children and a man called Billy Kestrel. We thought perhaps Billy and Myla would start a relationship, but they didn't. Billy had short-lived relationships with various women; Myla took up first with a Frenchman, René, then with Sheilagh's brother, Alan. But really Billy and Myla fell in love with us and we with them. Most nights they joined us in our room to listen to music and smoke. From time to time someone would go downstairs to make tea or fetch oranges. Night after night we assembled, Sheilagh and I lying in the bed, Billy and Myla sitting on the bed or on the sofa, rolling joints and getting high, listening to Coltrane and Reich, John Cale, Lou Reed and Bob Dylan until rosy fingered dawn came creeping round the edges of the curtains and it was time to sleep.

Sometime during my year of occasional writing they both moved out. First Billy, in the summer, to a small flat in Victoria bequeathed to him by the novelist, Rebecca Camu; then, in the autumn, Myla, back home to America. She had been on the road for two years, mostly living and working in India; now she needed to go back home, to resume half-forgotten relationships, to re-root herself. Life in that house had become too complicated. So Myla flew back to America and Billy went to live in Victoria and that Christmas I decided that I too must leave. Life was too complicated but also too easy. Something had gone wrong. Perhaps it was just that we missed Billy and Myla. But that Christmas I decided that I too must leave, must go away to write.

I would go to Ireland, land of writers. I would pack my suitcase, I would take the ferry and walk into the heart of Ireland until I found Yeats's tower, or one like it, and there I would set up my writing desk, without chocolate or whisky, and there I would write. I did not promise to become another Yeats, but I would become a writer. The days of putting one word after another purely for the sound or the beauty were over. I would write the story of my life.

I had to break the news to Sheilagh.

I took her to our favourite restaurant, an Indian restaurant in Horn Lane. Over the meal, my hand on hers, I told her.

'I have to go away, to write.'

'For how long?'

'I don't know. For as long as it takes.'

I was saying goodbye, though I didn't know it.

'You can stay in the house, of course.'

She didn't reply.
She said, 'When are you going?'
I said, 'Tomorrow.'

Did we make love? Probably. Our love was centred upon our love-making. Our first night together had consisted of eight hours of passion.

'I'll be back,' I said, or lied.

I took my heavy suitcase filled with clothes and books, my notes and a heavy old fashioned typewriter, went to Paddington station and bought a ticket for the overnight ferry to Cork. It was a rough crossing, salt sea spray blowing up across the deck and into my face as I sat out in the open, tears on my cheeks. Because I loved Sheilagh and seemed to have lost all reason. I went down to the bar and drank whisky and looked at the women in the bar and felt better. It was a long rough crossing. It was evening when I reached Cork, the evening of New Year's Eve. I found something to eat then went to bed and listened to the New Year revellers in the streets outside until at last, in the small hours, weary and exhausted, I slept.

Next day I travelled into the country by bus. I had no idea where I was going, knew only that I would find Yeats's tower or that my destination would somehow, mysteriously, reveal itself to me. I was heading north. The bus stopped in small towns and sometimes it was necessary to change buses. I sat on the side of the road near the bus stops watching children playing in the street.

I was little travelled. I marvelled that there were all these new worlds, so familiar and yet so different to mine. It was cold but the sky was bright and clear. Towards evening I looked out of the window of the bus and saw what I was looking for – a tower, seemingly in the middle of nowhere, stretching up tall and thick towards the sky. Whether or not it was Yeats's tower I didn't know but it would do. Here, I would be able to write.

I got off at the next town and tramped the streets until I found a woman kind enough to take me in. She showed me to a room. It had no desk and no heating – just a bed and a dressing-table at which, perhaps, I could write.

'Will you be staying long?' she said.

'I don't know. I will be in during the day, writing.'

'So, you're a writer?'

'Yes.'

'That will be fine,' she said. 'I won't disturb you. You can write here all you want.'

She closed the door and left me to it.

The town was called Fermoy.

The room was cold but through the curtains I could see the shapes that would eventually become my first novel, the novel that would make my name; and, beyond them, my tower.

I rose at eight-thirty and went down to breakfast. The house was not ideal for my purpose – I would have to attend breakfast each day by a certain time, my room had no heating and no desk, there was nowhere for me to go when inspiration ran dry – but I was tired of searching, tired of waiting. I couldn't bear the thought that I might carry on my search for the perfect place to write and never find it; that my life would become the mere quest for itself and unravel. So after breakfast I went upstairs and unpacked my typewriter and placed it on the dressing-table. The chair was too small and too hard, my writing position too cramped, but it would do. I unpacked my folder of notes, my typing paper and my books, put a sheet of typing paper into the machine and began.

After an hour my hands were chilled with cold. I stopped and looked out of the window. My house was close to the edge of the town and I could see green fields and hedges and cattle in the fields. I stopped work and went downstairs and knocked on my landlady's door.

'Would it be alright if I bought an electric fire? I will be happy to pay for any extra electricity of course.'

'Would that be a single bar or a double bar?'

'I hadn't thought.'

'It's just that the double bar would use more electricity.'

'Well, I could get a single bar. Or, failing that, I could get a double and just use the one bar.'

'Well, it will be alright so long as we keep an eye on the usage.'

'Thank you.'

I walked into the town to try to find a shop selling fires.

Fermoy is a farming town. In the middle of the town is the cattle market and opposite the cattle market a memorial to those from the town who gave their lives in the First World War. Just beyond the cattle market I found a shop selling second-hand goods. They had a single bar fire and a double bar fire. The double bar looked cleaner and so I bought it and took it home and plugged it in. Only one of the bars worked, but no matter. I was back on course. I stuffed another sheet of paper into my old-fashioned typewriter and resumed my work.

Every morning I wrote and every afternoon I walked in the lanes around Fermoy, marvelling at the greenness of the country-side, the height of the hedges, the wittering of the birds and the lowing of the cattle. I was little travelled. Sometimes I would see a young woman, maybe follow her for a while until it became too obvious or too awkward. I was filled with a young man's urgency, not only to write, to make a name for myself, but also to find my place in the world. I had left home early, when my father had died and my mother retired to a rest home. I had inherited just enough money to buy the house in London, the house where Sheilagh waited, the house that contained our one small room called Heaven.

Now I was in a strange place, without friends or family. In the evenings I would sit in my room and read or, plucking up courage, visit one of the local pubs. For whatever reason, the locals either fell silent upon my entry or made a show of ignoring me. The pubs in Fermoy were not like the pubs in Dublin, where a stranger might pass unnoticed. And, I soon discovered, there were no women in the pubs here. Fermoy was not that sort of town.

I rose later and later. More often than not, by the time I came down, my landlady would be on her hands and knees scrubbing the floors – she seemed always to be scrubbing and cleaning – and I would watch her as I ate, the folds of fat on her arms and legs quivering as she worked. My routine of sleeping in the day and working at night had become disrupted. I had been forced into working patterns that did not suit me. Worst of all, my tower had disappeared.

I asked my landlady.

'I saw a tower from the bus, as it approached the town. Is it far from here?'

She stopped scrubbing, there on her knees amidst the powerful disinfectant, and turned her head towards me.

'A tower?'

'Yes.' I attempted to describe the tower I had seen. 'It was tall...square...brown. Stretching straight up...completely on its own…no other buildings nearby...'

My landlady frowned.

'Well there's the Tower of Clonmashel – but that's fifty miles away, to the west.'

'It couldn't have been that.'

'There's no tower nearer.'

Could it be that I had seen the tower and then fallen asleep, that actually the tower was far from here? I didn't remember it that way. The way I remembered it, I saw the tower and then reached the town within ten or fifteen minutes. The way I remembered it, the tower could not be more than six or eight miles away.

'Are you sure? A square, brown tower, standing on its own, stretching up to the sky – about six or eight miles to the south?'

'There's no tower six or eight miles to the south,' said my landlady. 'At least not that I know of. And I've lived here all my life.'

'O.'

She returned to her scrubbing, I to my eggs and bacon.

I was writing about Sheilagh, Myla and me: quite deliberately, I was writing Billy out of the script. We had planned to travel, the four of us, with the children, but now my dream had changed. Billy would remain part of our lives but apart, in his own flat in Victoria, the flat he had inherited from the novelist, Rebecca Camu. We would arrange for Myla to come back from America, live together for a while, then travel. And my book was changing too. Whereas before there had been four characters, four of us on the mountainside, now there were three: Sheilagh, Myla and me.

I wrote in the mornings, sitting at the desk with the electric fire's one good bar blazing away beside me. I wrote in a rush, day after day, describing how it had been between us and how it was going to be.

In the afternoons, if it was not too wet, I walked. I walked the high-hedged lanes, past the wittering birds and the lowing cattle, each day a little further, to try to find my tower. I could not understand its disappearance. How was it possible that I had seen the tower so clearly – seen it from the bus, seen it even from the window of my room on my first night in Fermoy, vast and shadowy against the darkened sky – how was it possible that I had seen it and yet it did not exist? It was possible of course that, on that first evening in Fermoy, I had merely imagined it, that my first sight of it, seen from the bus, had somehow become imprinted on my brain. But I had seen it from the bus as clear as my own hand, as clear as the typewriter on my desk. I had seen it from two sides, from the south as we approached and from the west as we drove past it. But I remembered then, as I walked the high-hedged lanes, that there had been something strange about it: that however close we approached, the tower never seemed to get any nearer. Although the bus seemed to be driving straight towards it, the tower remained exactly the same distance from us; then, as we passed it on the west side, where it seemed the road would run beside it, it was as far away as ever. I had put it down at the time to a quirk of the land's geography, as a road might appear to run uphill when in fact it runs down. But now, I thought, it was more than that, something quite different. The tower could only be seen once – once, and never again by the same pair of eyes. But if that was the case, surely others must have seen it too? Surely even my landlady, who must once have lifted her eyes from her scrubbing, to see?

A little way ahead of me, as I walked, I noticed a young woman, walking in the same direction. Since my departure from England I had not spoken to a young woman of any description. There was little opportunity in Fermoy: no nightclubs, no meeting places, no young women in the pubs. This, I thought, was my chance. There was no-one to observe us; and the young woman herself could surely not object to a casual question from a stranger about such a significant landmark in the area of her own hometown. She was wearing strangely unseasonal clothes, a floral dress with a full skirt and a high collar and a short velvet jacket, and had a scarf tied round her hair; but her youth was apparent from the rapid, easy movement of her limbs. She disappeared round a bend in the road; I increased my pace in order to catch up with her but, as I rounded the next bend, found that she was no closer than before. I increased my pace again yet, however fast I travelled, the distance between us never diminished.

How can it be, I thought, that here I am, hurrying as fast as I can, and that she, walking at her own pace, remains the same distance from me?

And then I remembered the tower, how the tower too had stubbornly refused to get any closer, from whichever direction it was approached.

I walked past a field of cattle; some sitting in the grass chewing, others standing by the side of the road, gazing at me with their melancholic eyes. It began to rain, just a light drizzle at first, then harder, until the rain was stinging my eyes like pinpricks. A fine clean rain. As I rounded the next bend I saw the young woman, still the exact same distance ahead of me. Whether I slowed or speeded up, the distance between us never changed.

We were some way from the town. Normally by now, late-afternoon, I would have turned back as the daylight hours were short. But I decided to continue. The young woman must be going somewhere. It could be that she would reach an outlying farm, walk through the farmhouse door and close it behind her; then I would have no choice but to turn back. But there was something about her, the freedom of her gait, that made me think she was not a farmer's daughter. There was a long straight stretch of road ahead and I could see her clearly now. Again, I hastened towards her; again, the distance between us remained constant. But now, ahead of us, I could see a fork in the road: the road itself bending to the right, and a stone track that carried straight on, towards the wooded hills.

I was little travelled; in fact, apart from my visit to Dublin two years earlier, I had never before left the island where I was born. I was fascinated by the subtle differences between the English and the Irish. On the surface we were similar but the Irish had a different way of speaking, different nuances in the tone, different inflexions in the voice; different priorities, as it were, in their dealings with their fellows. They seemed more real, more relaxed, less uptight; would welcome you to their homes in a way the English never would. *We are here but for a short time and we never come again*; where had I heard this phrase? I couldn't place it but it seemed to sum up the Irish way of seeing things. A little less materialistic, a little less selfish, a little more present. It was no coincidence that the Irish were renowned for their love of music and poetry. Perhaps the Irish were selfish and insular when they needed to be; but they seemed to have a natural gaiety, a natural joy in living that the English lacked. Now, as the young woman turned off the road and set off along the stone track, I decided to follow. I had no idea where the track led, and, if it turned out to be a private track, little excuse for being on it; I could scarcely argue in my defense that I was following a young woman. But on the other hand I was a stranger, a tourist, out for an afternoon walk; was it so strange that I should detour off the main road in pursuit of recreation?

The young woman maintained her fixed distance ahead of me, a distance of about a hundred yards. The track followed the contours of the hill and quickly we were out of sight of the road. Now we were walking through a wooded area, with trees growing high on both sides of the track, and arching above us, so high they almost blotted out what little remained of the wintry sun. And yet the woman had not glanced round once nor broken her stride. That in itself was strange. She walked freely, purposefully, but never once looked round. She must know this track, I thought. She must be nearly home. And then she disappeared.

Every night I fell into a drunken stupor. I had stopped going out to the pubs; instead I purchased liquor at different outlets in the town and drank alone. Now, if I went out at night at all, I went only to walk beneath the full moon, picking up women's scent like a dog on heat. I followed a young woman down main street, up a hill, across a bridge, was about to call out to her when something stopped me. I did not wish to be recognised. I wanted to keep a low profile. It was true I had my afternoon walks but on my walks saw nothing but the brown eyes of cows, heard nothing but the wittering of birds.

I was writing about Sheilagh and Myla and how the three of us were living together in a small room called Heaven; my novel became a novel about my love for Sheilagh but also my love for Myla, her love for me and their love for each other. Billy Kestrel had become a peripheral presence, there only when I needed a break from the women (for all men, but especially writers, need a break from women from time to time). Each morning I wrote; but before I could write, hungover from the night before, I had to rise in time for breakfast. This had become more and more of an ordeal. My routine for years had been the routine of the night; these early mornings were leaving me tired and listless and I would be tired and listless from morning till afternoon; only in the evenings, when night fell, would I come alive. I would set my alarm for ten minutes before the latest possible breakfast time; ten minutes to rise and wash and dress and stumble down to the breakfast room. Invariably my landlady would be on her hands and knees, scrubbing and polishing the floor, though why she bothered I have no idea, as I was the only guest, and the floor seemed as clean before her scrubbing as after. In the early days she would pause from her scrubbing, sit up on her haunches and we would exchange a few words. How was the writing going? How was I enjoying the town? Now she didn't pause, just barked a greeting to the immaculate pungent floor and continued scrubbing.

'I found myself walking down a lane a few miles to the east,' I said to her one day. 'There was a track that forked from the main road and led into the mountains. A clear, well built, stone track. Could you tell me where such a track might lead?'

My landlady sat up, her arms covered in soapsuds up the elbows.

'Well, now, I'm sure I don't know of any such track.'

'It led into the mountains. It was where I thought I saw the tower.'

'Well, as I was saying…'

'And yet I saw it.' I paused and smiled. 'But perhaps I was mistaken.'

I decided to leave Fermoy; but on my last day, I would rise early, breakfast early, and walk back along the lane where I had seen her, take the fork up into the mountains and find her. It could not be impossible. Her image, like the image of the tower, was imprinted upon my brain. I would walk up the track into the mountains until I found her, or a trace of her, or her destination.

My landlady seemed surprised to see me.

'You're up bright and early.'

'Yes. Today I've decided to break my routine. I'm going to go for a long walk straight after breakfast.'

She looked at me sharply.

'O yes? And where will you be going?'

'Well, it's a clear day. Up into the mountains perhaps.'

'There are no mountains here.'

'No.'

She went away and I sat in silence listening to my breakfast sizzling on the stove next door. She came back and laid the plateful of food on the table before me.

'Well, you have a clear day for it.'

'That is all one can ask for.'

'Be careful though. The weather can change very suddenly.'

She left me then. I finished my breakfast and went upstairs to gather the few things I might need on my walk. I let myself out of the house and into the street. Everything looked exactly the same. I walked out of the town, along the lane where I had seen her, past the melancholic, ruminative eyes of the field-beasts, and followed the track towards the mountains.

# The Place of Departure

I went by minicab to the Place of Departure. While waiting for the cab to arrive I tidied up the flat – hoovered the carpets, secured the windows, turned off the central heating. Switched on the ansafone. I packed a bag (we were permitted a single bag): dressing gown, wash-bag, a paperback copy of *Tractatus*; forms (endless forms), together with a booklet issued by the Place for the use of new clients (it had a small, rather unclear map at the front, and explained in quite simple language the duties, and responsibilities, of both clients – they liked to think of us as clients – and staff); a pen and notebook; slippers, earrings; toothpicks; a Bible.

The driver arrived and sounded his horn. After a while he got out and rang the bell. I took a last look round – windows secured, ansafone on, TV and video off – stood in the hallway for a moment adjusting my tie, then joined him on the forecourt. I locked the door behind me. I went down the road to the mailbox to post a few letters, walked back, smiled at the driver, threw my bag onto the back seat and climbed in. I took one final look at the facade of the building where I had lived for so long – the slatted roof, the tall chimneys, the red brickwork, the lopsided front bay, cracked and tilting to one side – and wondered when I would see it again. I had grown to love that facade as one eventually falls in love with anything. Then we set off down the road, between rows of tall, smart houses, towards the common.

'Have we met before?'

He shook his head. He was a West Indian, Jamaican I guessed, in his fifties or early sixties. Doubtless he had come to England as a child or young man, carrying his memories with him like a suitcase. He was well-groomed and rather respectable-looking. His greying hair was neatly combed and brushed. He had a silver moustache and wore a pair of steel-rimmed glasses, which gave him an intellectual air. He smiled.

'I don't think so.'

'I just wondered.'

'No. I think not.'

We turned left opposite the common and queued for a while at the lights, then turned right along the west side of the common. The traffic was unusually slow-moving and there was a tailback at the lights just beyond the railway bridge. As we went through the lights I could see a funeral cortege a little way ahead of us with cars queued behind it. Beyond the lights the road widened. I pointed out the cortege. My driver looked surprised; clearly he had thought the traffic slow-moving for no particular reason, or perhaps no thought upon the subject had entered his mind. The drivers waited patiently out of respect for the dead. One car, a small white Toyota, suddenly shot out from the stream of traffic and tried to overtake the cortege. The driver put his (or her) foot down, the car screamed along the centre of the road but, just before the sports ground, was forced to pull in behind the lead car, breaking up the cortege. The cortege continued on its slow, dignified way with the Toyota sandwiched within it. My driver flicked a piece of ash off his moustache, pointed up ahead. Then suddenly he pulled out.

'The driver of that Toyota,' I said, 'is clearly mad.'

He pulled in again. It was a significant moment, a crossroads even, and I felt it as such. I knew then there was no going back. For a moment I was apprehensive. I glanced into the back of the car to check my bag. Somehow its presence reassured me. There were many things – my home, for instance – that I might never see again; but at least I had something left to remind me who I was, or had been. My little black overnight bag would be with me to the end. It would be there as I entered the Place, as I lay in my bed, as I slept, as I woke. It would be there the day I left. Its fate was now inseparable from mine.

The cortege continued on its slow way towards the river. We turned left into Cistercian Road, past an abandoned mental hospital where the ghosts of forgotten inmates still gibbered and howled. We all recoil from the stern face of death (except those of us who have fallen in love with it). But my new friend, driving slowly and methodically, brought us to the Broadway; then, after pausing for a moment, turned right and immediately left, into Kennedy Road, to avoid the lights at the main junction. In the distance ahead of us was a railway line that ran above ground, dipped under the main road, then came up again and ran alongside the Place itself (strange how our city is criss-crossed by this seemingly arbitrary network of railways). To our right was a small garage. A van flew down the road towards us. To my horror I saw that my driver was about to overtake a double parked car, which would have brought him straight into the path of the van. A tremor of fear ran through me.

It was my good fortune that my driver realised in time what was happening, braked and skidded to a halt. The van, driven by a long-haired youth with an ear-ring in his ear and a gold tooth in his mouth, swerved round the parked car and missed us by inches. My driver and I both ducked involuntarily, as though under fire. The van shot on down the road without slowing.

I shook my head.

'Mad as a hatter,' I said. Then, wondering if I had been tactless, 'Was he a friend of yours?'

'He was my brother,' said the driver; but, given that the van driver was a white man, and my friend a black man, I took this for a lie.

*the wheel turns round*
*the corn is ground*
*there'll be bread on the table*
*in the morning*

'Were you ever at the Place? I thought...you know...'

He laughed uproariously and shook his head.

'No. Not me, brother.'

'It comes to us all in the end.'

'Comes to us all in the end,' he repeated, tears of mirth streaming down his face.

I have taken, in my late middle age, to studying the faces of people in the street. Their haunted expressions never cease to amaze me. How rare it is to see a happy or contented face! They hurry by, pictures of misery, with their heads bent, avoiding my eye, as if some frightful calamity had befallen, or were about to befall, them. Sometimes, out of sheer compassion, I hail one of them: 'Hello, friend!' 'What's the hurry?' 'It may never happen!' 'Cheer up!' But they never answer. It is my belief that a man could become master of the universe were he able to tap into the secret of this despair and turn it to his advantage.

My new friend's laughter subsided, though he continued to chuckle sporadically. We discussed the concept of Time.

'Time is all we have,' he said. 'And not much of it.'

'Heidegger believed that time comes and goes in little eddies; sometimes future, sometimes present, sometimes past. Only we can't tell which bit is future and which is past.'

'Do we want to know, though?'

'When we reach the summit,' I agreed, 'we are obliged to throw away the ladder.'

My driver pulled out carefully to pass the stationary car, grinning at me. I noticed that he had a gold tooth in exactly the same place as the van driver.

*(Later)*

I glanced across at my driver, who was singing along to the radio. *When we have been there we kick away the traces.* I was feeling

48

quite light-headed. My driver turned and flashed me a smile, his gold tooth glinting in the grey light.

'I am not afraid of dying.'

'You lot never are,' he replied.

Ahead of us was a railway (strange how railways infest not only our city but our dreams: night after night I have dreamed of railways, of train journeys, of being caught in an open space with trains rattling round me from all directions, quite unable to move). He turned right into Trevelyan Road and drove parallel with the railway towards the High Road. On my previous visit to the Place I had parked in Trevelyan Road, walked across the High Road, along a side street, across the car park (always full, with signs both threatening and forbidding to those who had not mastered the peculiar intricacies of the ticketing system), through the remains of an old railway siding – where still, it is said, the ghosts of trains can be heard rattling through the night – and into the grounds of the Place. We drove to the end of the road, past yet another small garage (our city is littered with them) with its collection of double-parked second-hand vehicles for sale at prices that all ended, inexplicably, in *99* or *999*, along the side road where I had walked, until we reached the main gate. My friend drove past the first block, with its enticing entrances (Visit here! Visit us first! Welcome! Come in!), round the one-way system, then left towards the main entrance.

As always, the Place was a hive of activity. Members of staff in white coats hurried about, and clients (smarter and tidier than the staff in many cases) relaxed in chairs in little patio gardens, or were being wheeled from one of the many parking bays to one of the enticing entrances. The entrances had such names as Place of Delight, Place of Heaven, Place of Joy. My driver drove straight towards the main entrance – Place of Dreams – then stopped in the middle of the road.

'How much?' I asked. He waved me away with a smile.

I went through the main entrance and stood in front of the receptionist at the admissions desk. There were signs on the wall that said PLEASE GO FIRST TO THE ASSESSMENT CENTRE. There was thick glass between us. The woman had her head bent over a ledger. She was in her thirties, with short dark hair that barely reached her shoulders. There was a cup of tea on the desk. Another woman, a blonde with her hair done up in a bun and a cup of tea in her hand, stood behind her. She was chatting to a small, bald man in a green coat, who also held a cup of tea. From time to time they both laughed, and glanced towards the queue of people waiting on the other side of the glass. A third woman, the only other person in the reception area, turned and walked swiftly through a door at the back.

The woman continued to study the ledger. The blonde drank her tea. A tall, distinguished-looking man with grey tufts of hair sticking out over his ears walked slowly through the reception area beyond the glass looking towards the people on the other side. The telephone rang. The woman who was perusing the ledger picked up the receiver and spoke into it. She spoke so softly it was impossible to hear what she was saying. She made a note on a piece of paper that was lying beside the ledger then replaced the receiver. She resumed her intense study of the ledger.

A young woman walked through a swing door at the opposite end of the room and crossed the room towards me.

She smiled. 'Follow me please.'

She led me back through the swing doors into a wide, low-ceilinged corridor lit by artificial light, past another, larger reception area, and into a small room marked PHYSIO-THERAPY.

'Please wait here. You will be seen in a minute.'

I thanked her. She smiled again and left the room, closing the door behind her. The room was empty apart from a small leather couch, a small wooden filing cabinet and, beside it, a green armchair. I sat on the couch. After a few moments a tousle-haired young man came in. He spoke with a Scottish accent.

'My name is Dr McGanray. I am in charge of you. I can assure you it is a mistake.'

He cleared his throat.

'Have we met before?'

'I don't think so. May I sit?'

Without waiting for my reply he sat down on the green armchair and placed the clipboard he was holding on his lap.

'I must ask you some questions.'

'Why?'

'Questions are of the utmost importance,' he replied stiffly.

'Fire away then.'

'Good. Right.'

He cleared his throat again – it is possible he had a cold, or some minor throat infection – and crossed his legs.

'Right. Who are you?'

I told him my name. By way of elaborating, after a pause, I mentioned also my address.

'No no no,' said Dr McGanray. '*Who* are you?'

I had no idea what he meant. To make up for the apparent confusion I repeated my name.

'I was born in this very town.' I added on impulse, quite incorrectly, 'To a woman not known of man'.

'We get all sorts in here,' sniffed Dr McGanray. 'I'm afraid I will have to examine you.'

'I thought a mistake had been made?'

'That makes it all the more important.'

There was another, longer, pause. Then he said,

'There is nothing more important than importance.'

I took off my clothes and lay down on the leather couch. Dr McGanray examined me carefully, tapping me here and there with his fingers, listening earnestly through a stethoscope for my heartbeat, feeling my pulse. He peered down my throat with the aid of a small pocket torch. He squeezed my testicles, he tapped

51

my knees. He twisted my toes. Finally, with a sigh, he drew himself up to his full height, an absurd manoeuvre as his height was no more than five feet.

'What are we supposed to do?' complained the nurse in charge of the ward. 'I am alone on the ward. I don't have time to chase around looking for linen.'

The nurse who had wheeled me in, a plump, fresh-faced young girl, waited until the linen was found, then made my bed.

'You'll be fine,' she said. 'Don't worry about a thing.'

'When do you suppose the decision will be made?' I said.

'It could be today or it could be tomorrow. Or it could be postponed indefinitely.'

'And what will happen to me in the meantime?'

'You will be quite safe here. You won't have to do anything. Just lie in bed and read, or chat.'

I forbore to tell her that I had no wish to do either.

'Will you marry me?' I asked her, as much to make conversation as anything.

She smiled and soothed my brow. She leant down towards me and said:

'Yes of course, if that is your wish. You are in the House of Dreams now. The house where dreams come true.'

'And if I cease to be me?'

She laughed uproariously, tears of mirth streaming down her face.

'It doesn't matter.' She dabbed at her tears with an expensive linen handkerchief. 'It doesn't matter at all. No, no, not at all. There is no advantage in being you. It makes no difference at all.'

*(Later)*

My driver picked me up in the middle of the road. Everything was exactly as it had been. A gold tooth in exactly the same place as before. I climbed in and tossed my bag onto the back seat.

My driver opened his mouth in a great, gaping smile.

'Don't I know you?' he said.

He drove carefully around the one-way system, past the entrance block and out of the Place. He drove down the side road, waited for a moment at the lights, then turned left and right into Trevelyan Road. He drove, in stately fashion, to the end of Trevelyan Road and turned left into Kennedy Road. I noticed, not for the first time, the misery on the faces of the people in the street.

'They never answer. To their own gods or any other.'

We drove along Kennedy Road towards the junction with the Broadway. Near the junction there was a small garage, with a car double parked outside it. As he pulled out to overtake the car I saw to my horror there was a white van speeding down the middle of the road towards us. We had no time to move out of the way or even stop. The van hurtled towards us but somehow at the last minute the driver, a long-haired youth with an ear-ring in his ear and a gold tooth in his mouth, managed to swerve, miss us by inches, then shoot off down the road without a backward glance until he had vanished from view.

My driver was grinning from ear to ear.

'Takes all sorts,' he said. 'Where are you from?'

'I don't know. I was summoned to the Place, from where, as I'm sure you know, few return, but now they've released me with no explanation at all.'

'Don't worry,' said my driver. 'I was there myself once. They didn't want to let me go but I insisted. They let me out on a day release scheme, the days turned into weeks, the weeks into months and now…well, the rest is history. Still, where there's life there's hope, eh?'

'I wouldn't know,' I said.

# A Walk on Hoy

The girl's hair sliced back in the wind. She was walking fast in clean new boots. She overtook us after about a mile. We were hurrying for the last boat back to the mainland. I went on ahead and after another mile I found her sitting on a rock, cleaning blood from her face.

'What happened?'

'I have fallen.'

She was a hill-walker. She had walked these hills many times. These were not difficult hills.

Above us was the loch where earlier I had seen a red-throated diver on the water and great skuas flying in and out of the dark mountainside.

'Can I help?'

'It's alright.'

She looked down at her arm. There was a graze on her arm.

'Also,' she said, 'I have grazed my arm.'

She was German. She had come to Glasgow to teach German. 'As a language?' 'No,' she said, 'literature. And also I teach English.' She was a graduate of the University of Koln. She lived alone in a flat in Glasgow and came often to Orkney on walking holidays. She had walked this path many times before.

I knelt down and wiped the blood from her face. My companion arrived. I introduced her to the girl.

'She fell. She cut her head. She grazed her arm.'

The girl rose and we set off again.

'Do you walk here often?'

'No,' said my companion. 'But we have been to Orkney before.'

They were both teachers and soon fell into animated conversation. I walked behind them, past the loch (I could no longer see the diver). They were a contrasting pair: my companion slim as a boy in her tight jeans; the German girl stockier, wearing looser clothes, baggy shorts and an oversize shirt. She was more intense too, waving her arms about to emphasise each point.

A skua stared hard at me from a distance of about twenty feet from the track. I tried to signal to my companion that there was a good sighting but she was too engrossed in her conversation with the German girl. I watched the skua for a while and it watched me and then, when I turned back, the two of them had disappeared.

The German girl was called Agnes; she was meeting up with friends at the boat. They had driven together to the other side of the island and she was walking back on her own while her friends drove. 'These friends?' 'Girlfriends,' she said. 'Two girlfriends.' She laughed. 'They are not so used to walking.'

I wondered if she was a lesbian. Her dark hair, though thick, was cut quite short. She did not seem sexual at all, to me at least. Maybe to my companion. It was hard to tell. It is difficult for men to understand women, especially when they are not drawn to them sexually. They have their own interests, passions and artistic preferences. Whereas men prefer art that is absolute, women prefer art that is harmonious, in tune with their own lives.

To me, the skuas flying in and out of the dark mountainside were art, or would be were they stilled. But to them, their communication was more important.

Now they were gone. I searched through the binoculars but couldn't find them. Either the path dipped to create blind spots or they had walked off the path. Accidentally? On purpose? It could have been either. I don't know.

I remembered a story then, the story of my great-uncle, who went out one day into the South African bush and disappeared without trace. No skin, no bones, no mangled corpse. But, above all, no bones. The South African veldt is covered with bones but my great-uncle's were never found. He was, at the time of his disappearance, a boy of ten or eleven. Now he would be eighty perhaps. Perhaps he is still alive, the paterfamilias of a family that includes any number of little cousins of mine. They could be any-where – in America, back here in England or still in South Africa. *No bones* – so he could not have been taken by wild animals. But perhaps – it crossed my mind then – perhaps he was taken by some vast bird that bore him out of the territory, chained him to a rock and ate his liver.

It is, would have been, a sort of life. One would expect, natu-rally, to expire without a liver. But in this tale of mine the liver re-grew nightly and the bird came back each morning and ripped it out again, devoured it before the drunkard's eyes.

Dusk was beginning to slide in over the island from the sea and still I couldn't see them. I came towards the first traces of civili-zation – a gate, a fence, a stile. A huddle of dwellings beside the sea; a harbour; a jetty. The boat was there too, a simple passenger ferry with standing room only for the twenty minute crossing. I studied my companions on the boat but there were no two either who fitted Agnes's description of her girlfriends – no two young women from Glasgow in fresh boots showing signs of an absent companion.

# Keri-Jane

We drive to Andy's flat which is at the top of a tower block a few hundred yards from the station. The block looms above us like a dwelling positioned by the auteur of some space movie, unseen by any but its own inhabitants. Keri-Jane goes to fetch Andy while I wait in the car. At first I don't see him but then he is there, a few paces behind her: a gaunt man of my age or older with hollow eyes. We drive to a pub a few streets away where they've arranged to meet the dealer.

'I'm leaving my stuff here,' says Keri-Jane. 'Don't drive off, will you?'

'Why not take your phone?'

'No, I'll leave it. Just don't drive off, okay?'

'How long will you be?'

'Ten minutes tops.'

But they return straight away, the dealer's need this time as great as theirs. We drive back to the tower block and find a place to park.

'Do you want to come up?' says Keri-Jane. 'I'll only be five minutes.'

The sheet-metal lift shudders and groans, finally stops at the floor below Andy's. We get out and walk through a pair of heavy swing doors, up a flight of stairs, through another pair of swing doors. Andy walks ahead and unlocks the door to his flat.

The door has chisel marks as though someone has recently attempted a forced entry. Stuck to the door is a sign which reads 'If you don't know me I don't know you'.

The walls are covered in graffiti, traced montages, daubings on rice paper. The kitchen, cordoned off by a greasy string of cheap beads, is littered with unwashed utensils. We sit on cheap, stained sofas while Andy and Keri-Jane unwrap their purchases, find foil, heat up the powder and chase it round and round; little blobs of brown liquid mercury. Andy finds a tissue and rolls it into a tight string to soak up the residue.

'Andy's been to India,' says Keri-Jane. 'Two years wasn't it?' 'Two years in Singapore,' says Andy. 'What were you doing there?' There is a short silence. 'Andy paints and writes,' says Keri-Jane. 'He's had stuff published in Big Issue. Dig one out, Andy.' But Andy can't be bothered. 'I had copies,' he says, 'but I lent them to people and they never gave them back.'

'They're really good,' says Keri-Jane. 'He's really good, Andy.'

I've never met Andy before. 'I don't have any real friends,' Keri-Jane told me once. 'Just gear-friends, like Andy.'

I pick up a guitar and play *As Tears Go By*.

It was the first song the Stones ever wrote.

Andy looks up with vacant eyes.

'I'd like to learn that,' he says. 'Trouble is, I don't get any time to practise.'

'You have to practise. So your fingers know where to go.'

I show him the chords but his eyes are glazing over.

'I tried to text you,' Keri-Jane says. 'Did you get my text? I may have got the number wrong. We were doing it on Andy's phone and – well, you know what my eyes are like…'

Just then my phone bleeps.

'That's probably it now.'

But it isn't. It's a text from Vicky. I go to Andy's toilet to read it.

*Hi baby I just got ur message im at home down the road can I pop round 2nite please? I want 2 make up 4 lost time tb love Vicky x*

I reply: *2nite tricky, wil call u. James xx*

I pee in the bowl and pull the chain which, surprisingly, works fine.

The gear is finished. Keri-Jane kisses Andy on the lips. We walk back past the montages and the daubings. 'These are Andy's,' she says, pointing out colourful pictures of indistinct figures. 'Aren't they happy?' She is happy. She takes my arm.

'It's good to see you,' she says.

We walk through the swing doors and down the stairs.

'Andy's got a girlfriend who looks just like me. They call us the terrible twins.'

'Does she live with him?'

'No, but she's usually there. I don't know where she is tonight.'

We walk through the swing doors at the bottom of the stairs to the lift. Beside the lift, there's a hand-written sign stuck to the wall, put up by some of the residents, complaining of the lack of heating and hot water.

'They've had no heating for two weeks,' says Keri-Jane. 'No heating or hot water over Christmas.'

We wait for the lift. Keri-Jane looks at me and smiles.

'So you're speaking to Melissa again?'

'Yeah. My little sis. She's always having a go at me though. We had a big row just before I left.'

The lift comes. Keri-Jane slips her arm in mine.

'Where shall we go?'

'Home?'

'What about the boy?'

But the boy is not there, though his lights are on and the door to his room is open.

Keri-Jane takes off her coat and puts her rucksack on the floor in the bedroom. I roll a joint and pour some wine. She starts in on some story about her trip – how she went to the bus station with her brother Keith and they weren't allowed on the bus. 'I told him, "You're only a fucking road-sweeper, you fucking cunt". I told him straight – "you fucking cunt".'

'Can't you catch a bus without all these dramas?'

'I know. I'm sorry.' She tilts her head to one side, puts on her sweet face, pulls her chair up close. Puts her hand on my arm, looks up at me with innocent eyes.

'I love you,' I said once. She was on the end of a phone, on a beach in Weymouth, with her son Joseph and some other kids.
'I love you,' she said. 'Do you love me?'
'Yes,' I said. 'I love you.'
'There,' she said, 'there! You said it!'

We sit side by side on the bed while Keri-Jane spreads her foil and chases what's left of her brown powder.
'I don't like doing it in front of you.'
It's not the poppy that's the problem only the addiction.
A piece of foil flutters to the floor. Keri-Jane decides some of her gear has fallen too and starts searching.
I roll a joint and put my arm around her slender shoulders.
'You've got thin.'
'Me? No way.'
She lifts up her top and pats her belly.
'Look, I'm fat.'
'You're not, babe.'
We kiss, almost chastely. My mind flashes back to the first time, the first kiss, the kiss that changed everything.
I stub out my joint, tip back what's left of my wine and we roll into bed. I take Keri-Jane in my arms and kiss her again but her lips are dry and her eyes glazed. I steer her down to my cock and she sucks perfunctorily before sliding back up. I try to enter her.
'You're too dry.'
'O, I'm sorry…' but she's gone, half asleep, half in dream-world. I am too aroused to stop…I force my way in and start fucking. She relaxes, opens her eyes and looks at me. My face breaks into a smile and the words are there, hiding in the shadows, just behind my eyes. *I love you, Keri-Jane*. I close my eyes and come.

I open my eyes and look down at her. I kiss her dry lips and she kisses me back. She holds me tight and falls into a deep sleep.

# Bournemouth

We are lost, again.

'Babe,' I say, 'you must have come this way hundreds of times.'

'I know. I always get lost though.'

'What part of Bournemouth is it in?'

'There, there…left here!'

'Are you sure?' I say, swinging the van round.

'Yes. It's near Lizzie's.'

So we drive towards the shore, on the east side of the town, and then you recognise a road.

'This is it.'

'Are you sure?'

We are stuck in traffic, tailed back over a humped-back bridge.

'Yes, I know where we are now.'

You are unwrapping a cherrydrop. You are rolling a cigarette.

'It's the first right after the bridge.'

I turn right.

'O, this isn't it,' you say.

'Babe…'

I pull over.

'It's the next right. I'm sorry. It really is the next right. I know where we are now.'

So we turn and rejoin the traffic and crawl along a few more yards and take the next right and then we find it. A couple of low-slung warehouses with an office at the side. I ask you where to park.

'Park anywhere,' you say. 'There's no-one around.'

There's no-one around because it's lunchtime and the place is closed.

'What time do they open?'

'Two. They close for lunch.'

'Do you want to get something to eat?'

'Okay.'

We leave the van parked by one of the warehouses and walk out of the yard. There's a pub opposite.

'Where shall we go?'

'O, let's go to the pub.'

We enter the pub. There's little natural light, just the grey light through the window and the light inside from the low-wattage bulbs that angle up beside the vast mirror and the chandeliers hanging from the ceiling. I feel awkward, walking up to the bar with you, as though we shouldn't be here, or I shouldn't be here. I have never been to this pub before and now when I come it is our last day. Lizzie calls and you take the call and argue about who's to pick up Elijah from school and you hang up. I think, how many times have I called you and you've been in this pub and hung up on me?

'How are you two getting on these days?'

'Not very well, actually,' you say.

We stand by the bar in the dull light beneath the chandeliers. There is another mirror behind the bar and rows of glasses and upside down bottles of spirits, everything reflected in the mirror.

There is a man behind the bar and another man sitting up at the bar eating a piece of cake.

'I need to go to the toilet,' you say. 'I won't be long.'

'Do you want to order first?'

'I'll just have half of lager.'

'What do you want to eat?'

'O, I don't know. Anything. You choose.'

And you are gone.

A large, dark haired woman carrying three or four plastic bags in each hand comes into the pub and sits down at a table by the mirror.

'Alright?' she says.

Not really. How about you?

I don't know what you want, only that you're gone. Your mood varies from moment to moment. I've been with you when you've ordered chips and buttered slices and refused to eat at all. I've been with you when you've ordered steaks and sent them back because they were undercooked, lamb cutlets because you didn't like the sauce they were in. Taken bites from these and other dishes and given up.

'I was a vegetarian,' you say, 'for twelve years, remember?'

But how can I remember? You were a vegetarian before I even met you.

I order two lagers and ask to see the menu. I carry the drinks to a table by the window opposite the mirror. I sit down to study the menu. There isn't much. Sandwiches, paté, 'ploughman's lunch', quiche with salad. Perhaps they can toast the sandwiches. It is winter; perhaps I should drink whisky with my warmed-up sand-wiches.

There are sweets too: apple pie; ice cream; apple pie with ice-cream.

The woman sighs. Reaches for her handbag which accom-panies the plastic bags at her feet, lifts it by the strap, extracts a pack of cigarettes. She is not a lady of the streets, not quite. She has credit cards, cigarettes, a lighter. She fumbles for but cannot find the lighter. Sighs and turns, as if noticing me for the first time.

'Excuse me but have you got a light?'

'No,' I say, 'sorry.'

'It's a bloody nuisance, excuse my French, but I can't find my lighter. I was supposed to catch a train at twelve thirty but the bloody train left early. Excuse my French. Can you believe it? I'm on my way to see my daughter in Dorchester. It's not far, but too bloody far to walk.'

She turns to the barman.

'George, brings us a vodka, love. And a box of matches.'

And to me,

'The next train's not till half-past four. Are you alright?'

'Yes.'

'I'm not intruding?'

You are standing in the doorway. You are wearing jeans and a denim jacket and a big purple cap, which somehow matches your ginger-blonde hair and your child-blue eyes. You have a purple bag on a long strap slung over your shoulder. You peer shortsightedly around the room until you see me. You give me a shy smile. You walk towards the table and sit down. You never were the jealous type.

I show you the menu. Your phone rings. You squint at it, then answer.

'Hello? O. I told you, Lizz, about four. At the auction. At the auction! No I can't. Look, Lizz, I can't. I told you I would be. Yes, I did!'

You take the phone from your ear and put it on the table.

'She's hung up, silly cow.'

'What does she want?'

'She wants me to collect Elijah from school. I told her I couldn't.'

'She doesn't let up, Lizzie, does she?'

You open your bag to search for tobacco. You need a breather. You need to suck in the nicotine to clear your head.

I open the menu again.

'What do you want?'

You extract a cigarette paper and lay it flat on the table in front of you.

The bag lady leans her great weight towards us. Her stockings are in ribbons beneath the black skirt that rides half way up her thighs. She proffers her pack of fags.

'Have one of mine,' she says. 'I hope I'm not intruding? I was supposed to catch a train at twelve thirty. Now I'm stuck here for the rest of the day. Can you believe it?'

George arrives with the vodka, which looks like a double, and a pack of matches. He sets them before the bag lady and turns back towards the bar.

'Can we order?'

'O, sorry,' he says.

He is a small, thin man. He is wearing an open-necked check shirt and a worn grey suit.

'Sorry, I forgot all about you. Ha ha. What can I get you?'

'I'll have the paté.'

You have taken the menu from my hand and lifted it. Now you incline your head to peruse it.

'I'll have the apple pie,' you say at last.

'With ice cream?'

'No.'

But as he goes you change your mind.

You turn to me. 'Is that alright?'

'O,' you say, sitting back with your roll-up.

'Excuse me,' says the bag lady, 'but are you two on your way somewhere? I only ask because I couldn't get any sense out of them at the station. The train left early. Can you believe it? I hope you don't mind my asking?'

She is puffing out a cloud of smoke from her cigarette. Her white flabby legs, encased in their ripped stockings, are crossed, one above the other; her skirt ridden up above her knee.

'No, we're just collecting from the auction. They'll be open in a minute.'

'I know them. Very nice people. I hope you didn't mind my asking?'

'No.'

'My daughter lives in Dorchester. She's just got married. To a waste of space, as it happens. Now, of course, I have to travel all the way to Dorchester just to babysit. That's the reason they got married. That's the only reason anyone gets married these days, it seems to me. Are you two married? I hope you don't mind my asking. You look as if you are.'

I smile. It is our last meal together, our last few hours, our last chance to talk, sundered by this fat loquacious and probably lying bag lady, who thinks we're married, like a child from the womb.

'No,' I say.

And to you,

'Do you want another drink? I'm getting a whisky.'

'Okay,' you say, though your lager's only half finished.

'Same again?'

'Yes. Thanks.'

I get up ignoring the bag lady and walk to the bar.

'Cigarette?' she says.

What could we say anyway? Where would we begin?

Here, anywhere, nowhere.

Did we ever really love? I could spin that one round for ever and never reach the truth.

*Please don't leave.* I could say that. But that would have been a betrayal, of us, of everything, wouldn't it, babe? *Please don't leave.* But instead I say nothing.

A woman is standing behind the bar; a middle-aged woman with blonde hair done in an old-fashioned perm. She is wearing a yellow dress covered with red flowers.

'Are you the paté?'

'Yes, I'm afraid so.'

The thin man, her husband, is pouring a whisky from one of the inverted bottles on the wall.

'And he's the apple pie!' he calls cheerily.

'It's lovely fresh bread, fresh in this morning,' says his wife. 'Now, young man, what can I get you?'

'A whisky please. And two halves of lager.'

'Bells?'

'I'm sorry?'

'Bells? Or Teachers?'

'Teachers.'

'One Teachers coming up!'

The paté is sitting there on the bar, waiting to be brought over. I'd paid for the first round. Now, as I pull out my money, the woman says,

'That's alright. We'll add it to the bill.'

'So long as you don't forget.'

'Don't worry, I won't forget!'

I ask for a tray but she insists:

'No, no, I'll bring it over.'

Paté and fresh bread. I'd assumed the paté was served with toast but hadn't asked. But the bread looks good. The apple pie, I imagined, was still being prepared. I remembered the barman in Victoria treating us as though we were still lovers. What signs do they read? Do they sense the turmoil and come unerringly to the wrong conclusion? What is it that makes people want the best from everything as though there were no dark in the world but only light?

I carry the drinks back to the table. The woman in the flowery dress follows me carrying the food.

'Not that I've got anything against having children out of wedlock. I'd rather she had. It would have been better than marrying that waste of space and going to live in Dorchester.'

'O,' you say. 'Is it a boy or a girl?'

'It's a girl. Don't get me wrong. She's a darling. I love her to bits. Ha ha ha.'

She takes a great puff of her cigarette, leans back slightly and blows the smoke squarely into the middle of the room.

'I never thought I'd be a grandmother, though. Don't know why. Stands to reason, I suppose.'

'O, I love kids,' you say.

'Can't get away from it, can you? Got any kids yourself?'

'One. A little boy.'

'What's his name?'

'Elijah.'

'That's a nice name. Elijah. Yes, that's a lovely name. Elijah's chariot and all that. How old's Elijah?'

'Five,' you say. 'Nearly six.'

'O, the perfect age.'

You don't look up. I put down the drinks, push your fresh glass across till it stands beside the half empty one. The woman in the floral dress puts down the paté.

'The apple pie's on its way,' she says.

You are fumbling with your lighter, click click click. What is it with you and your lighters? You only have to look at a lighter for it to go on strike. For it not to strike. For it to strike against striking. You try to shield the flame with your jacket as though standing on the sea-front in a gale.

'Here, dear,' says the bag lady.

She is about to rise, convey her great weight from her arse to her ankles, but you forestall her. You slide out from behind the table, lean forward holding the cigarette in your mouth with your fingers. Your V-sign, peace, and with sudden recognition I remember who we are. Your long blonde hair falls in strands to your shoulders, one strand tumbling down beside the side of your face, across your ear.

You are half her size. You are half my size.

'I'd never go out with anyone who wasn't a real man,' you said.

You look edible in your denim and your big purple cap. Like a strawberry cake with a plum on top. Like an apple pie dolloped with rhubarb custard. You have an outsize watch on your wrist. I'd never seen you wearing a watch before.

You smile.

'Elijah gave it to me. It's only a child's watch.'

'Does it work?'

'No.'

You suck in the fire, lift your head and toss your hair back over your shoulder. You turn and walk towards me.

The phone rings.

You pick it up, scrutinise the display. Press it to your ear.

'Lizz? No, I said four. I can't. Because I can't! Because we have to go to the auction! Now. Now!'

Click.

'Well?'

'Stupid bitch. She wants me to collect Elijah, says she can't get off work without getting into trouble.'

'What about every other day?'

'O, I don't know. Sometimes he stays after school for his karate class.'

'But she must know she has to collect him today? Didn't you tell her we were going to the auction?'

'She probably thought I could be there by three-thirty.'

'How would you collect him anyway, without the car?'

'O, it's a nightmare, a nightmare!' says the bag lady. 'I'm sorry, I know I shouldn't butt in. What school does he go to? I hope you don't mind my asking?'

But you're sulking now, because of Lizzie and all the fuss. I spread butter and paté onto one of the chunks of bread.

'Do you want some?'

'No thanks.'

You smoke. The bag lady smokes. I eat. The bag lady watches us. She is going to speak. She sucks on her cigarette. She opens her mouth.

'I...'

You rise suddenly.

'I'm going to the toilet,' you say. 'I won't be long.'


Last night I dreamt about you, again. We were walking beside the river: you were crouching down, examining a dragonfly on a thistle.

'O, it's so beautiful!' you exclaim in wonder. 'I never knew the world was so beautiful!'

Like a child, snared by the world. Beside us the river is flowing: a heron takes off squawking, its legs dangling as it unfurls its huge wings and flaps slowly across the river to the safety of the far bank. Then we are on the path through the wood and there is a dog barring our path, a huge golden retriever, its great head lowered and swinging dangerously from side to side, snarling. The path is too narrow for the dog easily to go around us. He lifts his head and all you can see are his great white fangs, bared, dripping saliva. You turn and press yourself to me.

'O, I'm scared!' you say.

Suddenly the dog bounds past us.

'It's alright. It's gone.'

But it hadn't.

As we walked I heard, felt, the tremor of the earth as the beast turned and bounded back towards us, its fangs bared. I felt the fangs sink into my ankle.

'Run!' I called to you. 'Run!'

And you are running through the wood, swift as the wind. Then I am running alongside you and the dog bounding behind us. I know only one of us can make it. I call out to you: 'Run. Don't look back. Whatever you do, don't look back.'

'Get anything nice?'

'Excuse me?'

'O, I'm so sorry! You were miles away. Ha ha ha.'

She re-positions her thighs, flesh pressed to flesh, sucks on her cigarette, removes it, lets the smoke pour out of her open mouth: up, up into the room, where the smoke will pollute the air and the polluted air will rain down and poison us.

'Get anything nice?' she repeats, smacking her lips together.

'What?'

'At the auction.'

She nods her head towards the window and the low-slung warehouses opposite.

'I used to be in antiques myself once.' She rolls her eyes. 'Before *he* came along.'

How many vodkas has this woman drunk? How many cigarettes has she smoked? How many people has she driven crazy in her truncated life?

'No,' I say, smearing some more butter and paté onto the bread.

'O dear. That's a shame. What did you get?'

'A huge great fucking chandelier.'

'O, that is nice! I love chandeliers!'

The chandeliers sway above our heads in the currents of air and you are gone. Soon you will be gone for ever. I think of the old song, *Can't live with you, Can't live without you*, and think, That's us. But it's everyone else too. It's not a matter of can or can't. It's a matter of fate. We are victims of fate, that's all.

'Bring us another, George, will you, love?' she shouts, turning her head towards the bar.

Then she turns confidingly.

'I'm his ex, you know. He's a sweetheart, George. But a bit of a wimp, between you and me.'

Your apple pie arrives.

'O,' she says, looking around.

'She's in the loo.'

The woman in the flowery dress smiles. Then she says,

'How was the paté?'

'It was fine.'

'Good, good. Well, enjoy the apple pie! Can I get you anything else?'

She's a sweetheart, George's new one.

The room is full of George's women. But George, pleasant though he is, doesn't exactly look like a stud.

How do the two women relate? I watch them with curiosity but observe nothing amiss; no tension between them.

It occurs to me that the bag lady is a liar and a fantasist. She's no more George's ex than I am.

Now I catch her eye, and she uncrosses and re-crosses her legs and smiles at me.

'Your girlfriend's very pleasant,' she says. 'It is your girl-friend, isn't it? I hope you don't mind my asking?'

It is half past two. We walk across the road side by side, you don't take my hand, we're not lovers now, to the auction house. We walk into the yard where the van is parked. The warehouse door is open and we walk in. There's a Land Rover parked beside the van and a woman hurries up to us.

'Is that your van?'

'Yes.'

'Would you mind moving, so we can load? We'll only be five minutes.'

So I move the van while you go in to sort out the bill and I come in and it takes a while to sort out the bill because they think we're sellers, not buyers: the sellers, it seems, come to this auction house to collect their takings in cash. Everything is cash. At last they find our invoice and the woman behind the desk – just a window in the side of the warehouse fronting a tiny office – pushes the invoice through the gap beneath the glass pane that shields her from us and I take the invoice and read it then count out the cash and push it through the gap to the woman.

'Many thanks,' says the woman.

A man with a fino-pale handlebar moustache and a red-faced woman are ahead of us, loading up with silver. We hand the invoice to a black-haired man who waves his hand at the interior of the warehouse.

'Can you see them?'

'Can we see what?'

'Your acquisitions.'

'I dare say.'

'Come back to me if you can't, or if they're locked in the cabinet,' he says, and turns to the next customer.

The room is full of things I might have bought – stuffed birds, ivory handled walking sticks, antique sofas, modern hi-fi equipment, boxes of books. I start to peer into one of the boxes of books.

'I could have bought more,' you say. 'I didn't know how much you wanted to spend.'

'What did we buy?'

You are looking for a mirror and you can't find the mirror and you are about to go to the dark-haired man. There is a Georgian mirror perched on a Victorian chest beside the locked cabinet.

'Is that it?'

'No,' you say; then, upon closer inspection, you decide that it is.

'We could just walk out with anything.'

'I expect some people do. It's pretty laid back here.'

'Telling me.'

I pick up an ivory handled walking stick, test its weight.

'Illegal.'

'What's illegal?'

'This stick. Ivory.'

'It's not illegal.'

'It is. What else did you buy?'

We load the van piecemeal: the Georgian mirror, a fairy cluster mirror, a jardinière, a Chinese bowl, a collection of sticks (none ivory handled), an old sewing machine. It is difficult loading the van, fitting the pieces together so they won't scrape or topple. There is a pair of vases and a stone statuette of a dancing girl. They have no packing materials at this auction house. We find a couple of boxes, pack them as best we can.

'I also bought some jewellery,' you say. 'I hope you don't mind. We'll do well with it.'

The black-haired man scrutinises the invoice then leads us to the locked cabinet, which he unlocks with a key attached by a chain to his belt.

'Help yourself.'

'That's an invitation.'

'O, we know our customers.'

You find the pieces – a gold coin on a chain, a necklace, a pair of pearl ear-rings. The black-haired man finds a small box for them and we wrap them in tissue paper and drop them in. I stuff it in the back of the van, beside the jardinière.

'We'll do well,' you say, and turn to stare out of the window.

We are driving through the grey streets and already rain is splattering against the windscreen.

'Where does your sister live?'

You don't know. Though you know these streets your sense of direction is poor and you cannot find your sister's house.

'Ask these men,' you say, as we pass some workmen digging a hole in the road.

The conversation seems to go on for an eternity. You are attempting to locate your sister's house by the gradual revealing of clues – 'It's two streets away from a car showroom... I'm not sure, possibly Renault?... It's quite near the sea-front... There's a cul-de-sac leading off it, I forget what it's called...' The workmen, charmed by your looks and openness, are unwilling to let you go, forgo this opportunity not to work, though they haven't a clue, they aren't even from around these parts. And then, as we are driving off, turning, reversing, going back the way we came, I suddenly remember.

'We didn't pay for lunch.'

'Yes we did.'

'No, we didn't – we just walked out. I didn't pay. Did you pay?'

'No. I thought you paid. I'm sure you paid.'

'Well I didn't. We should go back.'

'No. They won't remember.'

Rain is splattering against the windscreen. You are staring out of the window trying to find your sister's house. At last you recognise it.

'Turn left here,' you say. 'And right at the end.'

In my mind I will embrace you. But you jump out quickly and walk away without a word or even a backward glance.

# The Literary Party

'Is that wine?'

She holds out her glass, swaying slightly. She is smiling at me.

'Do you want some?'

'Do I want some?'

'Well, I don't want to top up your glass without asking.'

'Why not?'

'It wouldn't be right. Without asking.'

'Why not?'

'You might not want any.'

'I do want some.'

'Okay.'

I pour wine into her glass, waiting for her to tell me to stop, but she doesn't. The deep red liquid bubbles up until her glass is nearly full. Then I lift the neck but continue to hold it poised.

She lifts the glass to her lips and takes a big gulp of wine, then starts to cough.

'Are you okay?'

'I'm okay. How about you?'

'Yes, thank you.'

'Wass your name, then?'

'James.'

'James what?'

'James Arachnid.'

'How do you spell that?'

'A – r – Look, does it matter?'

'Everything matters.'

'What's your name?'

76

'Steck.'

'Stack?'

'No.'

She transfers her glass to her other hand and starts writing in the air with her free hand. She spells it out in big letters: S T E C K. Steck.

'O – I thought you were a South African with a speech impediment.'

Her merry eyes regard me over the top of her wine glass as she sucks in wine with her teeth.

'I'm German.'

'O. Steck. I see. What does it mean?'

'It means baking tray.'

She emits a peal of laughter. Still holding her glass, the wine lapping at the edges and threatening to overflow, she doubles up. 'Baking tray,' she snorts. 'I'm a baking tray called Steck.'

'Well, I'm a spider.'

'A spider! Ha ha ha. Ha ha ha.' She waves her glass in my face. 'Hello Spider.'


'What do you do?'

'Me? O...various projects. You know.'

'No, I don't.'

'Well, I was building a well.'

'Why? You're a spider.'

'Spiders need wells.'

'No, they don't.'

'How about you?'

'I'm a freelance literary editor.'

She emits another peel of laughter.

'I'm a FREELANCE LITERARY EDITOR! Ha ha ha ha ha!'

'What sort of...you know...'

'What sort of you know?'

'Yea. What sort of...editing?'

'All sorts. I'll edit anything once I've had a drink. HA HA HA!'

'Would you edit a novel about snuff murder?' I say, topping her up.

'Yes.' She weaves towards me confidingly. 'Because, James, I'll do anything, absolutely anything, for a drink. Ha ha ha.'

Steck lifts her glass to her lips and pours the contents straight down. Like one of those birds you see on the tops of bushes with their little beaks wide open complaining furiously about the state of the world. You think you could just pop something in, anything, and down it would go and the bird would fly…

She holds out her glass. She is standing very close to me now and, as I tilt the bottle, directing the blood-red liquid into her glass, she puts her arm around my shoulders. I am big, Steck is small, but, even as I finish pouring, her arm stays put.

'Are you a snuff murderer?'

'No. But a friend of mine has written a novel called *Pig Bash*. About a man in Detroit who dresses up as a pig and kills people. No actually, other people dress him up as a pig and persuade him to kill people. He's an imbecile. It's quite complicated.'

'Doesn't sound very complicated to me.' She leans against me, turns her face to mine and begins to nibble my ear.

'My, you've got tasty ears,' she says, and doubles up again. 'Ha ha ha ha ha. Would you like to come back to my place?'

'Do you really want me to?'

'Why not?'

'Well…we've only just met, and…'

'And what?'

'Well. You're drunk.'

'I'm drunk?'

'Yeah. Fairly drunk anyway.'

'I'm not fairly drunk. I'm EXTREMELY drunk. Ha ha ha ha ha!'

'Okay. But…the answer is, in a word, or rather would be were you not, yes. Definitely. To discuss editing techniques, of course…'

'And then?'

'And then?'

Steck leans close and whispers into my chewed ear,
  'Shag.'
  'Well, if it was just a matter of shagging we could do it here.'
  'Let's do it here, then. Let's shag!'

We looked round the tent. The party was ending. The girls and boys behind the cloth-covered trestle table were already closing down. Mr Black and I had arrived late but he, being possessed of the gift of the gab, had charmed a last bottle from one of the pretty girls standing behind the trestle table amidst the almost empty wine buckets. Had engaged her in conversation while I had crossed to the other side of the tent with the bottle in my hand. Now he (and she) were gone; but there was a group of three quite erudite looking men standing quite close to us, all of whom wore black beards. They could have been anything or anyone. They were hard to tell apart.

Just then a young, sallow-faced man walked by and said,
  'Okay, Amanda?'
  'No, I'm not okay,' said Steck. 'This man wants to shag me.'
  'So shag him,' said the sallow-faced man, and stationed himself a couple of feet behind us.
  'Who's that?'
  'That's whoever-it-is.'
  'Is he your partner?'
  'My partner? Ha ha ha! No, he's not my partner. He's my brother.'
  'Your brother?'
  'No, not really. He's like a brother to me. He keeps an eye on me. Stops me misbehaving.'
  'Are you misbehaving?'
  'I don't think so. Do you?'
  'Not really. You haven't asked about me.'
  'I know all about you. You're a spider and you're building a well.'

'That's not all there is to know.'
'What else is there to know?'
'I'm a married man.'
'So, where's your wife?'
'Out of town.'
'Where?'
'I don't know.'
Steck leans towards me.
'Well, that's alright then, isn't it, Spider?'

We go round the back, stumbling over empty beer crates, into darkness. The moon is in shadow. The sallow-faced young man follows, hissing like a broken fly; behind him, in the darkness, the gaggle of blackbeards, murmuring.
'I do not think he knows what he's writing about.'
'He may. He may not. It really doesn't matter.'
'What concerns me is the inauthenticity on the page.'
'Truly, it is hard to believe such things happen.'
'At literary parties.'
'At literary parties.'
'At literary parties.'
Steck puts her hand on my cock and I feel my cock stiffen.
'My, what a big strong boy you are!'
She kisses me fiercely, pulling my head towards her, chewing at my lips. I slide my tongue into her mouth and she nearly chews it off. She unzips my fly. I hoist her up onto an empty beer crate and unbuckle her jeans.

# Hebden Bridge

I am travelling with a twelve year old boy, the son of my friend Jasson. Jasson has entrusted the boy to my care for a fortnight and I, in turn, have entrusted my daughter, Emily, to his. Jasson is a lawyer. We were at school together in the sixties and now, thirty years later, we are as close as we were then.

My daughter Emily is a little minx: she has a sign on her bedroom door which reads 'Bad Girls Say Yes'. She reckons she's a bad girl but she isn't really; just intemperate, a typical adolescent.

'Here he is,' said Jasson, as he delivered the boy to me. 'His name is Robert. Treat him well!'

'I surely will,' I said, and handed over my daughter, Emily. I embraced my friend and we parted. I looked behind to see the girl giving me that strange half-smile she sometimes gives when engaged in some complex system of lies.

We reached Hebden Bridge at midnight. 'I'd show you around,' I said to Robert, 'but it's late. We'll do that tomorrow. In the meantime, let's find something to eat.' But we quickly discovered all the cafés and restaurants in the town had closed. The only place we could find open was a club called Los Dos Diablos.

'Well,' I said to Robert, 'let's see if we can find something to eat here.'

Robert was a strange kid – autistic, Jasson reckoned, maybe dyslexic too, and half blind. No-one had fathomed him throughout his schooldays. He couldn't read or write but no-one knew why; he could converse easily with strangers but froze up altogether in the company of people he knew. Jasson reckoned it was his eyes – poor kid's three-quarters blind, he'd say to me, that's all it is; he can't see. But when they gave him optical apparatuses to use in school and sat him in the front of the class nothing came of it. The kid was still tongue-tied, still couldn't get his act together.

'He's simple,' some doctor said, but he wasn't simple. He could cut through to the heart of any matter.

'It'll do him good, to have a spell away from home,' said Jasson. 'He needs time to himself. Time and space – it's what all kids need.'

We entered Los Dos Diablos and found ourselves confronted by an enormous swarthy man, his shirt open to his navel, a vast gold medallion, upon which was embossed an image of Jason and the Argonauts, around his neck.

'Yeah? What is it you want?'

'We're looking for something to eat – me and the kid here.'

'Are you members?'

'No, we just want something to eat.'

'Well, you can't eat if you're not members.'

'Okay, we'll become members.'

'That'll be fifty quid each.'

'That's ridiculous. All we want is something to eat. We're not paying fifty quid just to come in.'

'So don't eat.'

I shrugged. I looked at the boy but he was looking straight at the enormous man with an intense look on his face. Maybe he hadn't heard the conversation. Maybe he didn't care. Maybe he cared too much.

I turned back to the man.

'Do you accept payment by card? I don't have that amount of cash on me.'

'Tell you what,' said the man. 'Give me an IOU and I'll let you in. What do you say?'

'Okay. Thanks. I'll come back tomorrow with the cash.'

'My pleasure.' He stood aside with a show of nonchalance and swept open a tawdry plastic curtain that shielded the inner part of the club from the foyer.

At first it seemed that there was no-one there. The room was in semi-darkness, all plush velvet, but tacky and tawdry. A waitress came up, dressed unsuitably in a skirt that barely reached the tops of her thighs and a flimsy golden kaftan-style top.

'You want a table?'

'Sure.'

'For two?'

'Yes.'

'Near the stage?'

'Really we don't mind. We want to eat.'

'I'll put you near the stage then.'

There didn't seem much point as there was nothing happening on the stage. I did notice though, as my eyes became accustomed to the darkness, that we were not alone. There were two men in business suits sitting a little way from the stage, and a couple – a tall dark-haired man with a prominent Adam's apple and his tiny fair-haired girlfriend – sitting right at the back. The waitress led us towards the stage and showed us to a table. The table was right beside the stage, so close we could have reached out and touched the performers, had there been any.

'This do?' she said.

'It'll do fine.'

'You want to eat?'

'Please. Could you bring us the menu.'

'There isn't a menu.'

'O. Well, do you have any food?'

'I'll have to check.' Then she reached down and stroked Robert's cheek.

'Who are you?'

'I'm just a kid,' said Robert, embarrassed.

'Yeah, but everyone's different,' said the waitress. 'You're not just a kid. You're you.'

'I know that.'

'So, who are you?'

He shrugged.

'I'm Robert. Who are you?'

'I'm Michelle. Do you think you could fall in love with me?'

'Maybe.'

She laughed, a pretty tinkling laugh, and let her hand fall to her side.

'You're a cute kid,' she said. 'I could easily fall in love with you.'

She turned back to me.

'What is it you want?'

'What?'

'To eat. What is it you want?'

'Do you have any eggs?'

'I doubt it.'

'No eggs?'

'You came at the wrong time.'

'So what do you have?'

'I don't know. I'll have to check.'

The waitress went away. I looked at Robert; he, in turn, was looking intently at the stage. 'There's nothing there,' I said in an undertone, but he said, 'Everything's there, if only you could see it.'

The waitress came back.

'Steak,' she said. 'We have steak. You want steak?'

'Okay.'

I turned to the kid.

'Robert?'

He shrugged. 'Okay.'

'There,' she said. 'All's well that ends well. How much did he sting you for?'

'Who?'

'The guy on the door. How much did he sting you for?'

'O, nothing. Just an IOU.'

I looked at Robert. He said nothing, just stared straight ahead.

'An IOU? He usually asks for fifty quid.'
'He did ask but we didn't have it.'
'You were lucky.'
'What's the show tonight?'
'What show?'
'Well – here we are sitting by the stage. There's a show isn't there?'
'There's a stage but that doesn't mean there's a show.'
'So there isn't a show?'
The waitress smiled.
'I didn't say that. I said, "There's a stage".'
'I can see there's a stage.'
'So, that at least we agree on.'
The waitress fluttered her eyelashes.
'Can I get you a drink?'

Next day we drove up into the hills to visit the artist, Marcus Jones. We drove out of town, across the bridge, span alongside the river and turned up into the hills. The boy sat beside me staring straight ahead. I looked at him but he did not seem aware of me. His mother had died, or run away, I couldn't remember which.

I wanted to break through to him.
'Do you remember your mother?'
'I do not have a mother.'
'Well, you did once. Your father's wife. She was a beautiful woman, kind and gracious.'
'I have no memory of her.'
He was literal all right. Jasson had warned me: 'He makes no emotional contact, but beware – he sees straight to the heart of things. You can't fool him.'

The clouds were lifting and from time to time the sun broke through. Huge black birds wheeled above us, crying shrilly. Jasson was a great expert on birds, and I had always thought I might become one too, for they seemed creatures quite alien to us, like flying fish...as close as we could come, I supposed, to what physicists call a 'parallel universe'. They had no need of us. There were few points of contact. I had no idea what type of birds these were – eagles, I supposed, or crows. Certainly they seemed like a premonition.

Now the sun burst through the cloud again, shining straight through the windscreen, warming us, as we climbed into the hills.

I had never visited the artist before, though his directions had been clear enough: 'Take the road from Hebden Bridge, climb into the hills until you can climb no further, take a left fork, follow the road for two hundred yards until you come to a track on the left. There's no sign,' he warned me, 'but a silver birch guards the track – you can't miss it.' (This was a joke I supposed, a take on man's credulity, for if there was one thing that united us it was a devout belief that we were aboard a ship of fools.)

'Do you have any cousins?' I said, knowing he had no brothers or sisters.

'What do you mean?'

'Do you have any cousins – do your father's brothers and sisters have any children?'

'My father has no brothers.'

'Sisters then – do his sisters have any children?'

'How would I know?'

'Well...do you not keep in touch with your family?'

'Why would I want to touch them?'

'I don't know...they're your family.'

'That woman, was she your wife?'

'What woman?'

'The woman in the restaurant that had no food.'

'O, the club... No, no, she wasn't my wife.'

The road had narrowed now and the hedges were high so the valley was hidden from view. The road was muddy and rutted, barely recognizable as a road. We came to the fork and I turned left and drove along looking out for the track. There was a track, but no silver birch; a little further along was a silver birch but no

track. It was typical of Jones, I thought, to play a prank. I wasn't
sure whether to continue or turn back.

The boy said,

'There.'

'What?'

'It's there.'

'What is?'

'The house.'

'What house?'

'The house you want to go to.'

And then I saw it...the track, with the silver birch standing
guard. But how had the boy known? Had I mentioned it? Had he
overheard me talking to the artist on the telephone?

But he was right, it was clear.

'Well spotted,' I said.

'What do you mean?'

'I mean...it was clever of you to see it.'

'I didn't see it.'

'No. But you did well all the same.'

'I did nothing,' he said.

We bumped slowly along Jones's track but there seemed to be
no house. We were in the midst of a wood now, the track only just
wide enough for the car.

We came to a fallen tree and could go no further. I stopped the
car and turned off the engine.

'What now?'

'We go on.'

'There's a fallen tree.'

The boy sighed.

'It's not a fallen tree,' he said. He turned to me, stared deep
into my eyes and slowly moved his hand across my face. I felt as
though I had awoken from a deep sleep.

'There,' he said.

I blinked and looked – the fallen tree was reduced to a pile of
leaves.

'How did you do that?'
'I did nothing. You can drive now.'

We came to the house, just a cottage really, two up, two down. The chimney exhaled smoke, chickens clacked and clucked in a little enclosure at the side. There was a barn attached to the house on one side – Jones's studio I guessed – and another, seemingly derelict, beside it.

I turned off the engine.

The boy turned his head. He was looking towards me but not at me...over my shoulder, as though there were some demon behind me.

'Are you frightened?'
'Why should I be frightened?'
'I don't know.'
'No, I'm not frightened.'
'You are.'
'I don't think I am.'

His eyes slowly focused on my face.

Marcus came to greet us. He was a short, wiry man, little over five feet, with an almost bald pate. He was wearing a pair of tight leather trousers, leather boots and white t-shirt which bore the legend 'Save Me Sister' above big bright drops of blood. I had known Marcus for some twenty years – almost but not quite as long as I'd known Jasson. He had started out as a painter, turned to writing, then abandoned writing for painting again. 'Novels and stories are for amateurs,' he said once, 'they rely on implausible plots and narratives when all you're trying to do is picture the world. With a painting you can cut through all that.' He claimed never to have sold a painting: 'The big-shots from London call me up from time to time but I'm just not interested. Why should I be? I don't need the money. Well, I do, but we manage without. I've all I want here. I hardly even go into Hebden Bridge any more.'

'This is Robert,' I said.

'Come and meet my women,' he said.

We followed him into the house. The house was small, two woodcutters' cottages knocked into one, the ceiling held up by old wooden beams and wooden pillars. A white Persian cat lay upon a state of the art hi-fi system in one corner of the room although, because little natural light came through the small windows, it was hard to be sure what I was seeing. Everything else in the room looked at least a hundred years old. An old sofa pushed up to a partition wall, beyond which lay an antiquated kitchen...a small wooden table and four chairs that might have come from the pages of Charlotte or Emily Bronte. Upon the sofa, before a table upon which rested two daiquiris and a book of Sylvia Plath's poems, sat two women. The older woman, Marcus's wife I guessed, had long red hair and wore a long velvet dress patterned in deep red and green. The younger woman had black hair, gathered and tied behind her head, a heart-shaped face, high cheekbones, green eyes. She was wearing a green latex corset that followed exactly the contours of her body, cleaving to her skin, cupping but only half-covering her breasts. She was wearing heart-patterned fishnet stockings and a pair of red high-heels.

The younger woman rose. She was five foot nine or ten at least, her height increased another two or three inches by her shoes.

She towered over Marcus and the boy.

'Chrissie, meet Robert...Robert, Chrissie...'

The boy seemed paralysed.

Marcus turned to me.

'Isn't she gorgeous?'

The woman smiled.

'Don't mind him,' she said. 'He's talking through his arse as usual. What can I get you? Coffee? Whisky?'

I looked at the boy.

'What would you like?'

The boy stared at her but did not seem to see her. Sunshine sparkled and span through the kitchen window and filled the room with silence. A silence unbroken even by the strange calling of birds. The woman put her hand up to her hair, unclasped it and shook it free. The woman with red hair rose from the sofa. She walked towards us, her hair shining bright in the dappled light, and held out her hand.

'I'm Elizabeth,' she said. 'Marcus's wife. I'm afraid Marcus lacks the grace properly to introduce us. I'm delighted to meet you. Any friend of Marcus's...'

The boy turned his eyes towards her. She cradled his head in her arms.

'O,' she said, 'what a beautiful boy. Who are you?'

'I'm Robert, son of Jasson.'

'I know that, I know that,' she cried 'but...who are you?

'I'm Robert, son of Jasson.'

'I must paint you immediately,' she said, 'before your beauty vanishes.'

·

# Iconography

*What are we? Are we just chemical-biological accidents or do we have immortal souls? Not one person living, or who has ever lived, knows the answer. And therein lies the clue (Teilhard de Chardin 1881-1955).*

We saw passers-by in the street – a man with a face pitted and cratered like the surface of the moon; a teenage girl, walking with a strange, shuffling, sideways gait, as though trying to hide herself from the world; a handsome young man in corduroy trousers whom at first you think is an upper-class loafer but later come to realise is an artist. You follow him. He walks with two female friends into a large house in the larger square that intersects with the square where Jane lives. The house is filled with artefacts – small iron sculptures, stylised Neolithic creatures, abstract paintings, objects that appear to be utilitarian but in fact have no practical purpose at all. The artist becomes increasingly agitated by what he sees. He tells his two female companions he must leave. He goes to a gambling club in Kensington and sits down at the blackjack table. Takes a blank cheque from his pocket, scrawls his name on it, pushes it across the green baize to a black-haired man with a face smooth as butter.

The man scrutinises the cheque. Turns it over to observe the back. Turns it over again to the front. Looks up at the artist then back down to the cheque then finally back to the artist again.

'Name?'

'Lockinge.'

'Well, Mr Lockinge, that'll do nicely.'

Lockinge does not reply. His mind is in turmoil. Everything for which he stands has been challenged and threatened by what he has seen: the useless exalted to a level beyond what is or is not useful.

He will lose. As much as possible, as fast as he can. Then he will be cleansed.

It is true that, sometimes, gamblers gamble in order to lose. But never before has this applied to Lockinge.

Lockinge exits the gambling club without even the money for a cab. It is after midnight. Three women come click-clacking down the street towards him. All are drunk. Their arms round each other's necks. Their pupils narrowed to slits. Their breath stinking, their speech slurred. Their clothes in disarray.

They stop in front of him because, being three abreast, there is no room for him to pass.

'Who are you?' says one of them.

'Lockinge.'

'Lockinge…' She says the name three times then starts to laugh. Her laughter is as wild as the night. As though the ancient forests were suddenly re-born and the earth become a dark and dangerous place, the continents sliding back together with a great clang.

She says,

'Wassyourname?'

'Lockinge.'

She breaks into a peel of laughter.

She says,

'WereyouliveLockinge?'

'Nowhere. I'm homeless.'

She eyes him up and down. Her laughing face turns to a scowl.

'You don't look homeless.'

'You don't look drunk.'

'I don't look drunk? Who are you, wassyername?'

'Lockinge. But you may call me Peter.'

Lockinge holds out his hand. The drunk woman takes his

hand, smiles tipsily, almost falls over, then with a certain grace raises Lockinge's hand to her mouth and sinks her teeth into it. Lockinge wails but she won't let go.

Lockinge's wails fill the terrified night. A night-bus rumbles by, slushing through the rain. It doesn't stop. The crazy woman's teeth are buried in Lockinge's hand. Teeth meeting through the flesh and weak bone. Bone too weak to withstand the bite. Lockinge is no athlete. He tries to tear his hand away but hasn't the strength. He wails and beats with his free hand at the woman's face. The woman's friends jump on top of him, accusing him of everything under the sun – rape, violence, GBH. They accuse Lockinge of attempted murder.

'Get her off my fucking hand!' screams Lockinge.

'Fuck you!' the drunken women shout.

One of them is on his back, her legs wrapped round his waist, like a jockey upon a horse. The other is halfway up his side, also with her arms around his neck, trying to sink her teeth into his ear. Lockinge feels the strength draining out of him. He gives up. His head spins once, twice, then he falls. He does not feel himself fall. He feels nothing.

Lockinge awakes. It is daylight. He is in the dry house.

A woman leans down and kisses him on the lips.

'Good morning, darling.'

Lockinge turns his head. The rest of his body, he realises, cannot move. He stares intently out of the window, at a plant seeded in the brickwork of the house overhanging the window. Thin, spindly branches, the bud, the small dry leaves. Heart-shaped, almost. The sun pouring down, lighting up the branches and leaves, pouring through into his dry room.

'Where am I?'

'Safe. Very safe.'

His pleasure receptors are tingling. He needs something which he cannot identify. He needs simultaneously to be stimulated and sated.

He tries to lift his hand to push back the sheets on the bed but instead pain rips through him, through his hand, his arm, and straight up into his shoulder. When the pain reaches his shoulder, he screams.

There is no-one else in the room. No-one hears him.

Lockinge winds his way down a wet road. On the side of the road are buildings made of glass and metal. The pavement beneath him is filled with rotten food turning to slime. He turns into the first open doorway he sees. There is a woman there, about thirty years old, with curly black hair and a ready smile. Good-sized breasts too, he notes with approval, beneath her tight jumper.

'Ten pounds,' says the woman.

Lockinge jerks up his head.

'Eh?'

'Ten pounds. To come in.'

'What sort of place is this?'

'What sort of place do you think it is?'

'A gambling *salon*?'

'No.'

'An art house?'

'Yes, kind of. You could say.'

'Okay,' says Lockinge.

'Ten pounds.'

'Okay.'

He puts his hand back to the back pocket of his jeans and pulls out a wad of notes. He peels one off. He hands it to her.

He goes in through a door of plastic strips. Inside there is an almost empty room. Metallic; functional. In the centre of the room is a spindly-legged table. Upon the table is an object, black, made of cast-iron. He goes over to the table and places his hand on the object. A woman steps from the shadows.

'You may not touch.'

'What?'

'You may not touch the artwork.'

'Why not?'

'Because if you touch it everyone will want to touch it.'

'That's not true.'

'O but it is.'

The woman is wearing a short tight pencil-skirt and a tight jumper. Beneath her skirt she is wearing black fishnet stockings. She is holding a pack of cigarettes in one hand, a lighted filter-tip in the other. Now she takes a slow draw on her filter-tip and blows smoke coolly into Lockinge's face.

'It's true, Lockinge. What you do the rest of the world will want to do. It's human nature.'

'No such thing.'

'O but it is, Lockinge. Didn't you know?'

He sees himself as he will be. Standing, his hand in his father's hand, outside the forbidden walls. Though whether he should stay or go he does not know.

# Michael and Issa

'I love I love you I love you,' she says.

Issa loves Michael. Michael loves Issa.

As though Michael and Issa were strangers to themselves.

Issa loves Michael. Does Michael love Issa?

'I'm tired,' I say. 'Will you let me sleep?'

I used to love Issa.

She begins to wail, her wails rising into sudden shrieks, subsiding, rising, subsiding. To the rhythm of her wailing, to the rhythm of the ocean, I turn for a moment to sleep.

There is a man standing before me with a sword in his hand. He says, quite clearly, 'I am the Son of God'. I smile – 'How can you be,' I ask, 'when, actually, I am?' But no, he is, I am not. Or so it seems. He waves his sword right under my nose and assumes horns and a devilish tail. His eyebrows grow till they meet in the middle, his bare feet become cloven hooves. He leans towards me and hisses,

'Who am I?'

'You are the Son of God,' I reply. (Wrath may be turned by a soft answer).

I awake and she is wailing. Her wailing goes on and on, so long it will reach out like a net and capture the swelling of the oceans, drag the salt sea ocean right across the city, through the window and into our tiny bedroom. Our bedroom is at the back of the house. I hear the first cars starting up in the car park. I fear her cries will shake the house down or at least draw attention to us. She may weep forever. Her weeping may continue until God knows when, until the sky falls in or the oceans rise up, to take us from one place to another.

Do the dead remember the living as the living remember the dead?

I look at the clock. We have set the alarm for eight and it is past seven. She rises and makes her way to the bathroom. She has stopped weeping. She wipes herself dry and flushes the toilet, brushes her teeth fiercely above the tiny sink. Water runs and the pipes rumble and hiss. Soon the whole house will be alive, guests rising and descending, breakfast in the breakfast room. Some here for pleasure, some on business. We came for an art exhibition though we needn't have come.

'One night,' she says. 'You couldn't even give me one night.'

'No,' I say. 'I'm sorry.'

'You're not sorry. If you were sorry you would have given me one night.'

'I didn't know what you wanted.'

Her wails cross through the thin walls that separate us from our neighbours. I should rise, I suppose, take her in my arms, tell her I love her. Tell her those half-truths and untruths that we must live by. We need only think ourselves happy to be happy, I would say, only think ourselves unhappy to be unhappy. But I do neither.

'Will you go down?'

'You go down, I'll follow.'

She is sitting at the cheap dressing table crammed against the wall, the table where once I wrote a broken verse, tore the paper to shreds and scattered them to the wind.

'Okay.'

I rise and dress. I wash my face in the half-blocked sink and run a toothbrush across the outer edges of my teeth. I look at myself in the mirror and see not a weary man with bloodshot eyes but a youth in the prime of life with golden hair and golden skin and muscles that ripple like water.

'You go down,' she says, as though nothing has happened. 'I'll follow.'

'I don't mind waiting.'

'No, you go down.'

My heart is as hard as a hardened artery, no blood flows through it. My hands and feet are like ice. My brain is a mollusc's, packed within impermeable rock.

Our friends are there – George Riyal, the artist, and his glamorous companion, LaConta. LaConta, squeezed into a tight tweed skirt, speaks in a whisper. Riyal sits with his son and does a crossword puzzle. I greet them. Riyal, engrossed in his puzzle, does not look up. LaConta whispers,

'Is Issa on her way down?'

'I don't know. She is weeping.'

LaConta smiles, brushes her foot against my leg. The boy, spotty and toothy, struggles for an answer his father knows.

# Lunch with Larry

'Now,' says Larry. 'Would you rather eat here or in the Frog? The Frog is very good, you see, but more expensive. The fixed luncheon menu in the Frog is £7.99 per person. Here…' he smiles primly and licks his moustache '…it's £3.99. And very good too. Mmm, yes. I can recommend it.'

'How about the Frog?'

'Well, of course, we *could* try the Frog. I'm told it's very good.'

'Or we could eat here?'

'Mmm, what an excellent idea. Yes. Mmm. Here it is then.'

A youth walks past us in the foyer and is about to vanish through a swing door when Larry calls out,

'We'll eat here, boy. Yes, mmm, we'll eat here.'

'Gotcha Larry,' says the boy, without breaking his stride.

'They know me here, you see,' says Larry, smirking. 'Mmm. Yes.'

'It's the injustice of it. Mmm. The sheer injustice. She is a creature of the devil. She is the devil. The devil incarnate. O yes. She's the one. If it wasn't for her I'd be there now. Between you and me, and of course I know we are of a like mind, mmm, yes, between you and me I can't even go there now. Because of her. Because of what happened. I'm a very sensitive person though people don't realise it. People come up to me and say, Larry, what on earth's happened? And I can't tell them. I can't say a thing. Mum's the word. Stew?'

'I'm sorry?'

'Stew. Or would you prefer the beef? Or, mmm, perhaps, the curry?'

'O. Well. Maybe…'

'Chicken, then.' He fixes his stray eye on the wall behind my ear.

'Okay.'

'Mmm, curry.'

'Well actually…'

'Good. Boy?'

'It's not him. It's her. He's fallen under her spell. Thirty-five years and this is how they treat me. Thirty-five years up in smoke! Lager!'

'What?'

'Lager?'

'O, yes. Certainly. Let me get these…'

'Mmm. Anyhow, as I was saying, it's so nice to talk to someone of a like mind. So few of us left now. Dear o dear. Anyway, as I was saying, so nice, yes, mmm. Where would one be without friends? I have a lot of friends. Dear, close friends. And admirers. So few, so few. Ignorant. Schools. You?'

'O, yes. I agree.'

'No, I mean…what will you have? A lager?'

'Yes. Let me get these.'

'Or the beef. Would you prefer the beef? Though you can't have the beef with lager.'

'No.'

'That's what I mean.' His wandering eye alights upon a space behind my head. 'Thirty-five years. And for what? Why?'

'Have you considered a book?'

'O, no. O, no. No, that's not me at all. I'm not a book person, you see. O, no. I'm a very… *people* person. Do you see? I have a lot of friends, close, dear friends. And admirers. And they all say the same thing: Write a book. But that's not me. What's the point? What? Boy!'

The boy, who is passing, stops. He is a spotty boy of about seventeen, with blue eyes and brown hair. A nice enough looking boy. He grins at Larry.

'Up for it, squire?'

'Mmm, what a cheek.' He squints at the boy. 'Pleased to see me?'

'Always pleased to see you, Larry.'

'Mmm.' Larry smirks and gives his moustache a little lick. 'Good. Now tell me, how is the beef?'

'Very well, thank you.'

'O, very droll, very droll. What I mean is, how is it? Is it good?'

'Impeccable.'

'O dear, you are an impossible boy. Very well. Beef for me, and my friend here will have the curry. By the way, have I introduced you to my friend?'

'I...'

'Well done.'

'What?'

'Well done?'

'Ah, I see. Yes, very good, very good. *Very good.* Yes.'

'So, that's one beef and one curry. Any extras?' The boy gives me a wink.

'Tch. Impertinent boy.' He turns his good eye back in my direction. 'Boys these days. You just can't get them you see. Anyhow. A pint of beer and a pint of lager. You will have a lager? Or would you rather have a beer?'

'Have a beer,' says the boy. 'The lager's piss.'

'Okay.'

'Two beers,' says Larry.

'Two beers and a lager.'

'Tch tch,' says Larry. 'Two beers. No lagers. And hurry up! Don't just stand there! You'll wear out the carpet.

'You just can't get them any more, you see. Fresh out of school and they can neither read nor write. Tch. What's this country coming to. Eh? Mmm?'


'So, now, tell me everything.'

'Well...people are horrified. Naturally.'

'Well of course they are. I am, why shouldn't they be?'

'Obviously your position is worse than theirs.'

'Of course. I don't mind admitting that. I've been quite low, actually.' He pushes out his pink tongue to bestow a quick damp brush across his little black moustache. 'You see, I've given them – him – my life. Since I was a schoolboy. Well, nearly. Thirty-five years. I was a young man in Surrey without any prospects and I wrote him a letter. It was my mother's idea. Just like that. Out of the blue. And two days later I was on a train to Pendragon and two days after that I was in his employ. In the Stable. Before the Limited. And now this… Sometimes I feel like…you know…'

'Well, if there's anything I can do…'

Larry fixes his gaze on my ear.

'What can anyone do?'

'Well, like I said, you could write a book, get the story out that way. I know you don't want to but don't dismiss it out of hand. You have thirty-five years' worth of anecdotes to tell. And friendly writers and editors amongst your friends…'

'Admirers.'

'Admirers. Or sue.'

'Sue?'

'Sue. Take him to court.'

'O, I don't want to do that! Think of the ructions! Dear o dear. Tch. Mmm.'

'But why not? They're spreading calumnies…'

'Are they?'

'Well, up to a point.'

'What calumnies?'

'Well…there are rumours. You know what it's like in a small town...'

'What rumours?'

'Well, that you…you know…'

'That I what?'

'Well, just that…obviously they have to justify it. So they justify it in the obvious way. Slanders.'

'Slanders?'

'Well, nothing exactly…precise. You know, innuendo.'

'Innuendo?'

'Well…rumours. You know. About you.'

'About me?'

We are sitting at the smallest table in the room though we are the only customers. Or rather the only visible customers for there is, or seems to be, another room at the back, from which sounds of laughter can be heard and to and from which moustachioed waiters trot bearing platters of pigs' heads, dead gulls and tureens of soup.

'Get away from the window!'

'What? Why?'

'O no, it's not that. Mmm. Not yet anyway. It's the sun. In my eyes.'

'But Larry, it's mid-winter. There is no sun. Only sleet and rain.'

The boy comes back with two pints of beer and a pint of lager. Larry glares at him.

'Foolish boy, you know perfectly well we didn't order lager! Two beers! Take it away!'

'Yes, you did. Two beers and a lager.' The boy turns to me. 'Isn't that right, governor?'

'I think we cancelled the lager.'

'No you didn't.'

'Yes we did.'

'Well, that's okay. If you don't want it, I'll have it.' He picks up the lager tips back his head and pours it down his throat. He smacks his lips, puts down the empty glass and wipes his hands on his trousers.

'There. Done and dusted. You gentlemen need any help with your beers?'

'O get away, boy,' says Larry smirking. 'Tch tch. Really. You're embarrassing everyone, not least yourself.'

'I'm not embarrassing me,' says the boy, and wanders off.

'Boys. I don't know. Anyhow, where were we?'

'Help.'

'O yes, help. Well of course…' his eyes narrow with furtive anticipation '…of course, I couldn't possibly accept any…'

'No. But a job perhaps. Or help with a book.'

'O no, no. Of course, I keep a diary. Who wouldn't? It's all in there.'

'So there is a book?'

'Well, not a book exactly.' He gives a triumphant smirk, pushes out his pink tongue to bestow a quick damp brush across his little black moustache. 'But perhaps the makings of one.'

'Well, Larry, that's wonderful.'

'Of course, it couldn't possibly be published before my death.'

'Of course not.'

'Completely libellous. Mmm. Yes.'

'Of course.'

'And Larry's not a book sort of person.'

'No.'

'But I have to admit that many of my closest, dearest friends, dear dear friends, inner-circle admirers, have made the same suggestion.'

'Yes.'

'Mmm.'

He lifts his beer.

'Well, to us!'

'Absolutely.'

He swigs. Froth clings to his moustaches. Out comes his pink tongue. Swish, swish, like rain-wipers in the snow.

# Crackheads

The man has a face like a clown. He wears a beret at an angle on his head and a pair of black-rimmed glasses. The glasses have no lenses. He is scratching his face determinedly: pushing up his empty glasses to get at his nose, massaging the flesh, pushing it and pulling it, then digging his nails back in. From time to time he places the heels of his hands above his eyeballs and wearily caresses them.

'How are you?'
    'You what?'
    'How are you?'
    His pale blue eyes alight lazily upon mine, squinting past the scratching hands, the caressing wrists.
    'Why?'
    'Could I buy you a drink?'
    'Are you gay?'
    'No. Why do you ask?'
    'Because you might be gay. I'm not going out with a gay.'

His hands high on the sides of his face like a pair of hands cradling a baby. A fluffiness about his lower jaw, an embryonic beard. Perhaps he is a follower of Trotsky; perhaps he, like me, believes in the re-distribution of wealth. For what is money but a barrier, a suit of armour, a mask? Life should be about breaking down barriers, not erecting them.

He has one finger up his nose, the other splayed on the side of his face: massaging, kneading, rubbing. His itchiness is deplorable. He must be a crackhead. His whole body is alive with itchiness. Itchiness seeps from his every pore, he is like a man in a state of extreme emotional excitation. But his voice is quiet and well-modulated and his face, despite its round, moon-shaped look and its fluffy Trotskyite beard, looks intelligent and not unkind.

'Why me?' he asks as he scratches.

His empty glasses are now perched on the top of his head, jostling for position with his jauntily-angled beret.

'I have all the money I need and yet all I feel is this wall around me,' I begin. 'It seems to me that in certain respects all people are the same. They have, at least, the same desires and uncertainties. What distinguishes them is only how they deal with it. But really there are only two ways of dealing with it – the way of aloneness and the way of being-with-others.'

'People let you down.'

I cannot place his accent – it seems at one moment Scottish, at the next Irish, all mixed in with a dash of Australian and a hint of Inuit.

We proceed along the court: a court ridden, I should say, with small bookshops and art galleries.

'Where are you from? Normally I am quite good with accents, but I cannot place yours.'

'Noocassel.'

His fingers now seem to be inside his eye sockets, scratching. I am fearful that his eyes, which seem quite blurry and blood-shot, will pop out. Observing my concern he suddenly removes his fingers from his eyes sockets and plunges them beneath his beret and into his scalp.

'You're a long way from home.'

'What?'

'Newcastle – you said you came from Newcastle.'

'That's what I said.'

'Do you not?'

'I've been all around. England Scotland Brittany Wales. How about you?'

'O, just London. I've never been anywhere.'

'Born and bred eh?'

'That's right.'

'And you want to go home?'

'No, I am home. This is my home.'

'Not any more it's not.'

'What do you mean?'

He taps his head and laughs.

'Up here,' he says. 'Memories. It's all we have.'

Halfway along the court he stops and stares into the window of a print shop. In the window there is a print of a bird, a falcon of some sort. The bird has a red belly.

'*Falco subbuteo*,' he says. 'Do you know why table football is known as 'subbuteo'?'

'No. Is it?'

'Yes. And all because of this amazing bird, the hobby. Table football is after all a hobby. The person who invented it wanted to call it 'hobby football'. But the phrase had already been patented so he called it 'subbuteo' instead. Clever huh?'

'Well, yes, I dare say. But of course, all he was trying to do was make money. Had he really cared about people...'

'Did people care about him?'

We are standing facing each other outside a shop that sells prints. My companion scratches the sides of his face, his head, the insides of his nose, his eyeballs. Suddenly, without warning, he plunges his hands into his pants and launches an assault on his genitals.

'Do you want some crack?'

'No. Why do you ask?'

'You seem very itchy – you look like a crackhead.'

'Well I'm not,' he says, beavering away down below. 'I'm not a crackhead.'

Crack. It makes you feel good but the real appeal of crack is not that it makes you feel good but that it renders you out of your head. Where is the charm in that? It is obvious that the people to whom crack most appeals are those who do not like being inside their heads or even inside their skins. Dancers and musicians take crack and they seem comfortable inside their skins, at least when they are dancing or singing. But deep down something is wrong. You know something is wrong. You know he did not just suddenly start taking crack and like it so much he went on. No: it was an urgent necessity for him to get out of his head. And crack fucks you up...so your head, after a lengthy course of crack, is really no place to be.

'Well,' I say, 'that's sorted.'

'Sorted,' says my companion and laughs, showing red, itchy gums. 'Yes, everything's sorted.' His hands are deep inside his pants now working their way along the sides of his droopy scrotum, around the insides of his thighs, then stretching through to the foothills of his buttocks (an approach from the rear might have been the better option). His eyes redden and glaze over and I know it is only a matter of time before he must return his attention to his face.

'Everything's sorted. O yes, that's a good one. What's next?'

'Well,' I say, 'I'd like to try crack myself. Just so I know what it's like. Not to become an addict.'

'Ha ha ha,' he replies, nails digging into his flesh. He is a comical sight, with his trousers unbuttoned, his hands deep inside, clawing feverishly, shirt-tails flapping. Pierre Broulée, the owner of the print shop, notices me and waves. I am a regular customer, perhaps he thinks my companion is soliciting alms. I feel I need to explain the situation to Pierre for Pierre has been a good friend to me, finding me rare prints, giving me first refusal on items for which he must have had a string of customers. Pierre gives me a feeling of reassurance for, unlike me, he seems quite happy with his life, or if not happy at least content. I have no idea why.

'Come and meet my friend Pierre,' I say to the fellow.

His hands come out of his trousers and I gasp: his nails are red with blood.

'See what crack does to you?' he says, waving his hands in front of my face.

'It's not the crack that's fucked you up but the addiction.'

'What would you know about that?'

'Look, I'll give you some money, money for crack, if you like.'

'What would you know about that?' he sneers, as though he were God incarnate.

Pierre, alarmed no doubt by our discordant body language, comes to the door of his shop. He smiles briefly at me then turns towards the scratching man.

'You again. Fuck off,' he says.

'Anyone for crack?' sneers the Geordie.

'Go on, fuck off,' says Pierre. Although not particularly large or aggressive Pierre is as ferocious as a terrier when he wants to be.

'You cunts are all the same,' says the Geordie. 'You want to help with this, you want to help with that, and then, when the going gets tough, you fuck off out of it back to your money-world. Your money-in-the-nursery-world. Money is a web, a cocoon. It's official. Once you're locked in it, you can't get out. Fuck you. And fuck you too,' he adds, turning to me.

'I was only trying to help.'

'Well,' he sneers, 'I don't need your help. Your help means nothing. Wankers like you do more harm than good. You want to know the secret of life?' He tapped his head again. 'It's up here. Goodnight.'

'Sanctimony. You're proud of your habit because it's all you've got. You hated your life in the first place, then you hated your addiction, then you ended up proud of it because it's all you had left to be proud of. It's a fucking tragedy.'

I think for a moment he is about to take a swing at me but stand my ground.

'Waddye ken? What d'ye fucking ken?' he says, his accent

switching suddenly to Scots. 'I'm free as a bird.' He projects a glob of phlegm at my shoe.

'Fuck off,' says Pierre Broulée, though it's not entirely clear whom he is addressing.

'Aye, that's it,' says the crackhead. 'Only language you fucking cunts understand. You're all the same. Fucking cunts.' And he sticks one hand down the back of his trousers and the other through his empty glasses straight into his eye.

# Sylvia

'High above us, up on that hill,' said Marcus, 'is Sylvia's grave. Everything we do here, you might say, we do for Sylvia.'

The younger woman comes back carrying a glass of whisky. She holds it out to me looking into my eyes. She releases the glass just as my hand closes round it. The glass falls at our feet and shatters.

Marcus looks at the young woman and she smiles back at him. She goes away, returns with a dustpan and brush, kneels at my feet to sweep up the broken pieces.

The two women walk hand in hand to the top of the hill and stand before a windswept open grave. 'O,' the red-haired woman cries, 'what has become of my beloved?' The other woman strokes her hair. 'Hush now,' she says, but quite emotionlessly, like a nurse soothing a troublesome infant. 'But they've taken her!' the older woman cries. 'They've taken Sylvia! They've stolen her away! O, what will become of me?' The other woman seems distracted almost to the point of inattention. 'O, I don't suppose she's gone far,' she says. 'But can't you see...she's dead?' 'She's not dead,' the other woman says.

Then they are silent.

But the earth spins faster than we think. We get used to it, that's all. If it slowed or stopped we'd develop headaches or vertigo of the sort we feel when we step off a child's merry-go-round and find the earth still moving beneath our feet.

'It is what it is!' cries the woman, as thunder crashes and the skies split and a snow-storm roars and swirls and envelopes her.

'What is what it is?'

'Everything!'

The other woman becomes attentive to her now, cradling her head in her arms, stroking her hair. 'Hush,' she says. 'It will be alright. She'll be back. Sylvia will be back.' The distraught woman slowly calms, sinks into the other woman's breast, puts her arms around her neck and pulls her tight. 'She will never come back,' she says, holding her. 'None of us ever comes back. That is the end of it.' And the snow storm swirls and covers them up as though they had never been.

# Tuning the Guitar

He tuned the guitar, adjusting the three top strings until they were in tune then tuning the others to them. He played some chords, getting the feel of it; he tried different keys until he found one he liked and played a song. She watched him and joined in, singing loudly. At the end she said he would have to teach her that song. He showed her some more chords and chord sequences, jumping between different shapes, showing her all he knew. Her eyes began to glaze and she leaned back on the bed: 'You are going too fast, you forget I am only beginning.' He explained the formations again and played snatches of various songs. He showed her how to structure a song and asked her to choose any song. She sang *Black is the colour of my true love's hair* which he played in D. She enjoyed singing but he was getting restless. He played a song she didn't know and she watched him. 'Do you like that?' he said. 'Yes, you are very good.' 'No, not really, I am out of practice. I was never any good really, that's why I gave up.' He played some scales, running over the keyboard. 'Stop,' she said, 'I am tired. You are showing me too much. You know the instrument but I am only beginning. I cannot follow all this.' He was carried away now, in love with the instrument. She lay on the bed. 'Stop,' she said. He began to play a rhythm in three time. 'You must learn about rhythm,' he said. 'That is the most important thing when you are playing a song, more important even than the notes.' She lost patience, full of frustration with him, jealous of the guitar. 'You are not trying to teach me,' she shouted. 'You are just enjoying yourself. You are a useless teacher, you are just doing what you want to do.' He smiled sardonically. 'Yes, I am enjoying it. What's wrong with that? I haven't played for a long time. It wouldn't be much use trying to teach you if I didn't enjoy it.' 'You are not trying to teach me,' she shouted hysterically. 'You are just trying to show off all you know. You know perfectly well I can't follow in five minutes what you've learnt in ten years. You are just selfish, horribly selfish like all men. All you want to do is enjoy yourself. You understand nothing of women.' He put down the guitar. 'I am not trying to understand women, I am trying to show you some of the things that you can do with a guitar. I was trying to show you different rhythms.' 'Different rhythms,' she said, 'different rhythms. How long did it take you to learn different rhythms? Ah,' she turned her head away, 'you make me sick, you are just like all the others, you understand nothing.' He grinned at her. 'Do you want me to go?' 'Do what you like,' she muttered. 'Go.' She pulled off her clothes and got under the sheets. He took off one shoe, and stood up. He walked around the room. He sat down on the bed again. 'Shall I get into bed?' 'Do what you like,' she said. He took off his clothes and got into the bed. 'Turn the light out.' 'Why don't you?' 'Turn the light out.' He got up and went to the door. He stood naked, suspended for a moment then, with a flourish, clicked off the switch. He lay down in the bed facing her and put his arms around her. He ran his hands over her body. She did not respond. 'You're not getting it,' she said. 'I have my panties on and there's nothing you can do.' He continued caressing her. 'It's no use trying to turn me on,' she said. 'I don't feel like it.' With a half repressed sigh he rolled over and sat up. He reached for a cigarette. 'There,' she said: 'you're bored. You only come here for one thing and now that you aren't getting it you're sorry you came.' 'Do you want me to go?' he said. 'Yes,' she said, 'go. That's what you want to do, isn't it?' He sighed. 'I just don't like spending the night away. It interferes with my routine.' 'Go then,' she said. 'You're too late for the bus.' He lay comfortably in the bed, smoking. She leaned over and took the cigarette from him, sucked on it, gave it back. 'I am not like you think,' he said. 'I don't have many friends. I hardly ever sleep with anyone. I haven't slept with anyone since I last slept with you. I need my routine and my solitude. I don't particularly like getting drunk.' 'Now,' she said furiously, 'you are feeling sorry

114

for yourself. You haven't got what you came here for and you are sulking. Just because I won't cuddle you and let you feel me where you want to. Tch, you are all the same; if you can't get what you want you sulk like little boys. You are all too sensitive and talented to understand anyone except yourselves. Ha! You make me laugh. I'd just be interested to see if you like me enough to spend the night here without screwing.' 'Yes,' he said. 'I thought that was the game.' 'Game?' she said. 'Who's playing games? You think I'm playing games?' She laughed unpleasantly. 'You're the one who's playing games, with your, o yes, shall I come back and teach you guitar, o yes, is it alright if I come back and sleep on your floor tonight – what did you ask me that for if you're so worried about your routine? – o no, let's not go for a drink, I don't like to get drunk – well you liked it well enough before and now you don't even respect me enough to get drunk when you come to see me! O yes, you are a fine one with your games. You are just a little baby boy who wants mummy to cuddle him. Well go and find someone else to cuddle you.'

'Well now you see,' he said wearily, 'why I don't have many friends.'

'O fuck off.'

'You wouldn't be hurt if I go?'

'Do what you want.' She turned to him and put her hand on his thigh. 'You may as well stay. It'll save you the taxi fare.' He thrust towards her with his body, pulling down her pants with his hand. She stiffened. They lay like frozen statues. 'I'll be tired all day tomorrow. I shouldn't have come,' he said. She did not reply. 'No, I shouldn't have come. I didn't even particularly want to come.'

He got up and dressed on the darkness; looked down at her pretending to sleep.

'Goodbye,' he said.

# Cable Street

In the city I found the hotel. The Travel Inn. I asked for my brother by name at the reception. The man to whom I was speaking had receding hair and a large moustache. He looked like a professional wrestler, or maybe a soldier. He reminded me of my father.

'Why are you searching for him?' he said gravely.

'I have something for him.'

'A gift?'

'Not a gift.'

'A weapon?'

I looked at him more closely. I could see the resemblance to my father, or rather the father I never had. He was grave, wise, fair, stern.

I walked south, through Chelsea, to Greenwich Village. In Washington Square I listened to the guitar players, watched the chess hustlers fleecing the city kids. One of the hustlers asked me for a game.

I shook my head smiling.

'Not me, man.'

'You, man.'

He stared straight into my eyes. He was an Hispanic, with tough, dark eyes and a bandana round his head. Though behind his eyes I could see he was vulnerable.

'Okay.'

We sat down. He sat, I noticed, with his back to the sun. I played white. I shuffled my pieces around to create confusion. He brought out his queen too soon, retreated to the wrong square. He picked up the piece to put it on a better square.

I put my hand on his arm.

'Touch move.'

'Touch move? Okay.'

He put his queen on the bad square allowing me to win a pawn. After that he played to win on time. I forgot the time. I had the sun in my eyes.

'I'm looking for my brother.'

'Why?'

'Do you know him?'

He put his hand on my arm.

'Why?'

I picked up the money.

'There's a street in SoHo,' he said. 'Off Cable Street. It's a taverna, a sort of strip joint. Do you like girls?'

I walked up and down the street. The street was deserted. I found the strip joint. There were pictures of naked women on the door.

'You like naked women?' a woman asked me.

I sat at a table. On stage a tall woman took her clothes off and lifted her arms. There were half a dozen other people in the room. The naked woman walked around the room inclining her breasts towards the men. When she came to me she said,

'You looking for someone?'

'My brother.'

'Give me money.'

I put some money in her belt.

She lifted her arms and moved her body from side to side in front of my face. I smelt the sweet fragrance of her skin.

'Come back at midnight,' she whispered.

I walked out of the strip joint and walked around the deserted streets for a while. At each junction there were couples looking for taxis, only taxis were hard to find. A young woman passed me on the cobbled street walking a black dog on a string. I asked her for a light.

'Sure.' She stopped, put her hand in the pocket of her coat. Pulled out a gun.

'What do you want?'

'I'm looking for someone.'

'Who?'

'You wouldn't know him.'

'Why'd you speak to me?'

'Shouldn't I?'

I looked towards the end of the street, down towards Cable Street. Even now there were a few people walking on the street.

'Do you live around here?' I asked her.

'Sure.' She lifted her eyes towards a building at the end of the street.

At midnight I went back to the strip joint. I sat for a while watching as the stripper finished her act. She lay naked stretched out on the stage simulating intercourse with an imaginary lover. Her garter belt was full of money. She stood up, lifted up her arms and bowed. She went backstage to dress. She came back out to the front dressed in her street clothes.

'O, you're here.'

We walked to Cable Street, took a cab to her apartment in Tribeca. She lived in a loft at the top of the building. The loft was full of life-size sculptures. She took off her coat and fixed me a drink.

'He was here,' she said. 'He stayed here for over a year.' She nodded towards the sculptures.

'His?'

'Yes.'

'You are his brother?'

'Yes.'

She poured me another drink.

'You can stay here,' she said. 'But you sleep alone.'

She slept in a small room at the end of the loft. It had nothing in it but a bed and a telephone. After she had gone to bed I walked around the loft looking at my brother's sculptures. Some were of people I knew, people we'd both known from the old days. Some were self-portraits. Others were of people I didn't know. There were several of the stripper.

# Skallion

Carrying our possessions we walked rapidly from the house to the street. Skallion walked three paces behind me, a bag in each hand, his crop-head lowered, his small eyes swimming within their pools of thick glass. We turned left into Steep Hill, crossed the road and carried on up towards the street. We reached the street and passed the coffee shop on the left where sometimes on Saturdays Skallion would meet the crazy man to play chess. The crazy man couldn't really play chess but thought he could. He started a chess club which had only three members: himself, Skallion and a nameless Indian who didn't play but liked to watch.

The street was thronged with indeterminate humanity and Skallion soon found himself by my side.

'Do you still play chess with the crazy man?'

Skallion began to reply then fell silent.

We couldn't catch a bus from the usual place because the council had embarked upon a pavement-widening exercise, though the pavements seemed wide enough, and had fenced off whole areas of the street, forcing all traffic into a single slow lane and inconveniencing everyone.

'Councils,' I said to Skallion. 'Bloody fucking councils. We won't miss them.'

Skallion began to relate the story of a reprimand he had received from an elderly relative for upsetting a younger cousin.

'When was this?'

'When they were young,' replied Skallion.

'When who were young?'

'Christopher and Tommy.'

'How young?'

'Seven.'

'How old are they now?'

Skallion, faced with a question he couldn't answer, had only two responses: to remain silent or to stutter. He began to stutter.

'I-I-I... I-I-I...'

'You don't know?'

'I-I-I...'

There was a bus ahead that would take us part way to our destination. 'Let's catch it,' I said. I ran forward with my bags, Skallion following, but just as I reached the bus the driver closed the door. I rapped on the door with my bags in my hands but the driver ignored me and drove off.

'That's what it's come to, Skallion,' I said. 'Men cannot live like this.'

'They want to take the park,' added Skallion.

'Who?'

'The council.'

'Why?'

Skallion fell silent. He stared down at the concrete pavement.

'Let's find a cab,' I said, though in truth we had no money for a cab. All we had were our bus passes and our possessions in four bags. We had placed within these bags our most treasured possessions but in the end the selection became random. What is treasured varies from moment to moment. Which is more use to a starving man, a piece of bread or a Bible? Or, for that moment, an expensive watch? Time doesn't matter. Time may be revealed by the rumbling of a stomach, a growth of beard or desuetude. I wore three days' growth, Skallion two. Skallion shaved occasionally but randomly for he could not see his face in the broken glass.

Another bus came and we stepped onto the raised platform, put down our bags and began searching for our bus passes. I found mine in the left pocket of my jeans and placed it upon the device by the driver's window. It pinged twice, once red once green. Skallion could not find his then remembered it was in a bag within a bag. He must open both his bags to search inside. Other passengers embarked, pressing their passes to the device, stepping over or round us. At last Skallion found his card but as luck would have it it pinged red then red again. A young woman climbed aboard and pressed her pass to the device which also pinged red. She entered anyway. Skallion and I picked up our bags.

'Not in,' said the driver, staring straight forward through the glass.

'Eh?'

'Not in. Not him.'

'No, it was the girl who pinged red. He pinged green.'

'No money on the card.'

He wasn't threatening, just staring straight ahead as though his mind were fixed upon other things. Tea-time, perhaps, or the heat, for the heat had risen like flies from a swamp, grasped us and was attempting to drag us down. Wisely Skallion and I had most of our clothes within our bags rather than about us.

'What?'

'No money on the card.'

'So what do you want?'

'Money.'

'How much?'

The driver named a sum.

'Alright,' I said. 'But this is daylight robbery. We are leaving this town but not, it seems, before you and your kind fleece every last penny from us first.'

The driver said nothing. I pushed the money through a small hatch beneath the bullet-proof glass that divided us. The driver took the money without turning his head, pocketed it, and jerked the bus into gear. 'Watch out, Skallion,' I said. 'This guy will just pull off without giving us time to find our seats.' We went upstairs. I directed Skallion with his bags to the front seat. I sat one seat back across the aisle next to a foreign girl with a mobile phone pressed to her ear. She spoke softly in, I guessed, Polish.

On and on it went, call and response, without laughter. The bus lumbered forward, stopped, turned at an acute angle then lumbered forward again.

'Now we are on our way,' I said.

The bus stopped, started and stopped again. Repeatedly it stopped and started. It pulled itself tightly up to other similar buses as though trying to copulate with them. A cyclist was hit by a lorry swinging left onto the South Circular Road. At each stop a seductive female voice called out the name of the nearest road or park, sweet-talking us through the inferno. Four young men climbed onto the top of the bus shouting and laughing and spilling cans and the contents of cans across the floor. They went to and fro, switching seats, putting up their feet and laughing. One of them shook up his can and sprayed the contents into the face of a blameless passenger. Another walked up and down the bus reaching across the heads of the passengers and banging the windows shut. Another followed to bang them back open again. Closing or opening like oyster shells engaged in a cosmic dance. Laughing till tears streamed down their faces.

Tiring of the game they went noisily back downstairs.

The bus reached its terminus.

'We are here,' I said.

Without a word Skallion picked up his bags and stood up. He stretched slightly, the bags in his hands, and yowled like a wolf at the moon.

'Here,' I said. 'We've made it.'

We disembarked. Stepped onto the burning pavement where they walked, the beautiful, the ugly, the free and the damned. A drug-dealer caught my eye and hissed like a rat. We stood on the side of the road waiting for permission to cross. An illuminated man came, flashing and pinging, and we crossed with the others and were swept down into the entrails of the town. We were out of money though such was our fortune I still had some credit on my bus pass. We found a way through the barriers and carried our bags down to the staccato train.

'We are here,' I said to Skallion. 'Soon we will be there.'

Skallion did not question me further for he knew that our destination was unknown. The face of the driver expressed horror and incredulity as the train poured into the station and shuddered to a halt yowling and hammering. We climbed onto the packed train. A youth stood in the middle of the carriage a rucksack on his back and a guitar at his side, clinging to a strap and swaying as the train pulled out. He had come to this town, like Dick Whittington, to seek his fortune. Here his life would be, and the ones he would meet and the ones he would die for. Everyone needs to be the one less ordinary except those who would foster and nurture. A man in a blue suit stood clutching a brown briefcase. A young woman sat intently and made up her face in a hand-mirror. At every stop the doors opened and some exited and some entered. The young man disembarked in the centre of town. I smiled at Skallion. He stared at me blankly, his eyes swimming discoordinatedly within the thick pools of glass.

'Soon,' I said, 'we will be there. Gone and forever gone.'

Skallion put down his bags, scratched beneath his arms, then hefted them again. His head bowed, his hair sliced into a 'number one' and the scars on his neck plain as day.

# Beside the Sea

'Are you there, man?'

I hear his voice, earnest, uncomprehending, straining. Where was I? I had no idea. I knew I had fallen, for miles it seemed. I knew the cliff had given way, a fissure had opened and I had fallen into some sort of cave or tunnel.

I strained to hear his voice through the darkness but all I could hear was silence.

Then, drifting on the wind, a song about flowers. It wasn't until it was nearly over I realised it was a parody, a vicious satire – not a song about flowers at all.

There was more to him than I could understand.

I was clinging to the ledge; could move neither up nor down.

I did not like to ask him to rescue me.

I looked up shyly.

Now, balanced on his even more precarious ledge, he was rolling a joint.

'Kim,' I said.

He seemed not to hear me.

'Kim!' I said more loudly.

He paused, the cigarette paper raised to his tongue. Looked down. I realised with fear that he could not see me.

As though I had slipped into a different time or place.

He was listening but the only sound he could hear was the sound of the sea crashing on the rocks below, rolling in like giant fingers, plucking anything within its reach into its fathomless heart.

I thought, Will you pluck me too, with your giant fingers, into your fathomless heart?

'Kim!' I shouted but my words were lost in the roar of the wind and the raging and crashing of the sea.

Now the light is in my eyes and another voice is talking. A woodentop, his hat sticking up to the sky.

'Whose car is this?'

I have no idea.

Then I remember a girl I know, Marika.

'It's Marika's.'

'Who's Marika?'

'A girl I know – from London.'

The woodentop regards me from beneath an arched eyebrow.

'London, eh? You're a long way from home.'

'Yes.'

'When did you start this journey?'

'Some time ago.'

'How long?'

'I don't know – a few months.'

'In this vehicle?'

'Yes.'

The woodentop says nothing, just continues to gaze at the paperwork spread out on the desk in front of him. Was there something there that contradicted our story? The meaning was eluding me. Words like 'years' or 'months', what do they mean? How can we measure time? Time exists within us, like the rings inside a tree. It cannot be measured until the tree falls.

A mad notion struck me – that the world was created on a particular day, a day with a date, and came into being exactly as it was, with all the fossils, all the evidence of natural selection, already in place.

Can time run backwards? Perhaps it does. Does time 'run' at all? Or is it that 'time' simply 'is'?

Our existence is the only evidence for our existence.

Time is motion. Time is the not-being of what once was.

'Right,' he said, 'that's it. You're nicked. No tax or insurance.'

I looked at Kim and he looked at me.

We burst out laughing.

'Give us a break,' I said.

'And,' he added, 'as you cannot prove you own the vehicle, with taking without consent.'

Kim looked at me. I looked at him. He was about to fall in a heap.

'Taking without consent?' I said. 'From whom?'

The woodentop allowed a slight smile to caress his grim features. One side of his mouth moved towards what could have been a dimple in his cheek, the other remained; as if he had, at some stage, been disfigured in a fight.

'That is for you to decide.'

'Actually, it belongs to my mother,' I said.

It was hard to take it seriously. I couldn't distinguish between reality and dream, or dream and dream, between rival dreams, optional realities. Kim had a theory about parallel worlds he'd read in a book. It made perfect sense to me. Take the officer's hat, swap roles. Why not? Neither version is more or less real than the other.

'Have you visited London?' I said, to break the silence.

His smile quickly faded, slowly faded, until, as hard as I looked, it was no longer there.

He knows no fear. Wearing plimsolls, without ropes or crampons, he scrambles up any rock-face leaving me trailing in his wake. He runs up rock faces like a wild goat.

He landed beside me on the balls of his feet.

'I used to climb rocks all the time when I was a child.'

'Yes, but not stoned, presumably.'

'O no, man – ganga makes me strong!'

Just don't look down…

I followed him up the cliff face but in the end I gave up. He was two ledges above me, rolling a joint.

'Where now?'

He pointed upwards. 'Come up,' he said. 'Or' – he pointed downwards – 'down'.

I turned to look and my heart rushed into my throat, jolted back down into my stomach at the fall.

# Fishergirl

I knew a girl called Lulu. She used to visit me in my flat in London but at times of her choosing, not mine. I would return from a journey, of days or weeks, and within hours of my return I would hear the clunk of the letterbox and find a hastily scribbled note lying on the mat. 'Hi how r u ITS LULU.' 'LULU here just passing, call me?' Or she would text me from her mobile phone. Sometimes, wherever I was, she would phone me. 'Hi, it's LULU, just wanted to know you okay, don't speak, don't talk, just wanted to know, it's LULU bye!'

I came to think she was a little crazy.

I travel a lot – partly to get out of the city, which discomforts me but which I cannot live without, partly in the course of my work. My work is unusual in that it consists solely of exploration. Sometimes my explorations are what the gurus of the sixties, Huxley, Leary and the rest, would call 'inner space voyages'; explorations, that is to say, where I delve deep inside myself, chemically, spiritually, until I reach a place I do not recognise and stay awhile. Other times my explorations are external. I travel the world looking for new landscapes, new rock formations, new types of terrain, and stay until they have imprinted themselves on my consciousness. I have been to Australia, America (north and south), Africa, most places in Europe.

When I was younger I preferred the gentle cathedral cities of Europe for my explorations: now I seek wildernesses. The most beautiful places on earth, it seems to me now, are not cities, however gentle, but the arctic tundra, the forests of South America and the great red deserts of Australia.

My religious acquaintances tell me I am, albeit unwittingly, seeking God. I tell them that there is no God…though I readily acknowledge that the impulse for their explorations is not dissimilar to mine. We are all seduced by the impossible; we all wish to shake off the shackles of our earth-being.

Or she would simply ring the bell. I grew familiar with the sound of her high heels click-clacking on the pavement outside my house. I knew instantly it was her. She walked in a way no-one else walked, with a rare determination and single-mindedness. Click clack click clack click clack click click, right up to my door. I would hear the bell in my head before she even rang it. I would open the door and there she would be. Standing there, quite shy despite her single-mindedness. Sometimes I would barely recognise her. I had an image of her in my mind – a tall, strident, black-haired woman, with black eyes and dark skin, a beautiful, lustrous creature, her passion rising, her lips thickening with blood. But standing there on my doorstep she was simply a lost child of no more than medium height, her curly hair cut short, a shy smile on her face.

'It's me, LULU,' she would say. 'Are you pleased to see me?'

Sometimes I was and sometimes I wasn't. When I wasn't – should I be, for example, in the middle of writing up one of my explorations – I would simply dismiss her.

'Lulu, I'm busy. Come back in two hours.'

'Okay.'

She would turn on her heels and walk quickly away, click clack click clack. Sometimes she came back two hours later, more often not. Something had come up. She might come six hours later or two days later. But she always came. Always the bell would ring and she would be there.

'It's me. LULU. Don't your recognise me?'

'Yes, I recognise you.'

'So, can I come in?'

'Okay.'

She was always well dressed – low cut jeans with a big belt, or a pretty green dress with silver boots. She would look around the flat as she entered to see what I had brought back from my latest exploration. It might be a shrunken head, dry bones or a daub of wattle. It might be an ancient text or a piece of modern music.

She would sigh and plant herself in the nearest armchair.

'I have been having a terrible time.'

'Have you, Lulu?'

'I don't know where to begin. I don't even know' – and she would give me a fierce look – 'I don't even know if I should tell you.'

'Tell me or don't tell me.'

'Okay, I tell you.' And the tale was always terrible. She had been on the way to the airport to fly home for her children's birthdays when she was mugged and had her ticket stolen and had had to return instead to her bleak lodging room in London. Or she'd found herself a nice flat and paid the deposit, everything was arranged, and the landlord had stitched her up and rented the place to someone else. Or her benefit cheque had been stolen and she had been penniless and hungry for a week. Or, worst of all, she had been raped.

'Raped?'

'By a black guy.'

'How come?'

Slowly the story would emerge. She had invited this guy back to her room because she was lonely and he seemed like a nice guy. He too was an artist, she had been to his studio to see his paintings. She liked his work. He had invited himself back or she had invited him, it wasn't clear. He had come back with her and they had spent the evening together and then she was tired and asked him to go but he wouldn't go. He just sat there in the chair. Then he went over to her CD player, turned the music up to cover her cries and raped her.

But she did not seem especially perturbed by this and gradually the story changed. Yes, she had allowed him to stay the night

– it was too late for his bus home. She had allowed him into her bed. She had got into the bed with him. She was naked. He was naked too. And he didn't actually rape her because she had her period…instead, bizarrely, he insisted on eating her blood-soaked pussy.

'So how come this was rape?'

'Well, I made a mental decision to allow him to do whatever he wanted in case he tried to kill me.'

'Did he threaten to kill you?'

'No.'

'Did he behave violently at all?'

She would smile brightly then…she had said enough. She had told her story, had drawn me in. Now she would change the subject. 'What about you, James? Where have you been?' And I would tell her – New York, Australia, Bremen, wherever. I would tell her of the voyage out, and what I'd found, and the voyage back, until her eyes glazed over and she fell asleep in her chair.

I felt sorry for Lulu. That she was lonely was obvious – why else would she choose to spend so much time with a wanderer like me, why else invite these strangers to her bed? She claimed variously to be a political refugee, in flight from an abusive husband, a morphine addict, an addict to prescription drugs but, apart from her erratic schedule, there was no evidence for any of this. I might take out a new CD I had acquired on an exploration to, say, Mali, and she would get up from her chair and dance. Sometimes she would dance for hours. It seemed to provide a release for her. Sometimes her dance would turn into a strip-tease and, at the end of the dance, she would be standing there naked.

'Now,' she would say, 'you want play with LULU?'

Other times she would quickly pull her clothes back on and leave the flat in a rage. 'You exploiting LULU: you like all the rest.'

I said to Lulu, 'I'd like to take you on one of my travels. We've been spending time together, why not? See how it goes.'

131

'You want see how it goes with LULU? Boy, you crazy. You not know?'

'We've never travelled together.'

'Travel at the heart of DISASTER.'

'Why?'

'Because Lulu knows.'

'To travel is not to arrive. At disaster or anywhere else.'

'You ever been to Portugal?'

'No, why?'

And she would smile a secretive smile. 'You want know why? You want know why Lulu talk about Portugal? Because LULU PORTUGAL.'

'You are Portuguese?'

'No. Listen. Lulu not Portuguese. LULU PORTUGAL.'

Her texts became crazier:

*James its better 2 keep yr mousse chut.hot batata*
*not burn y. bye! LULU*

*Faith I make my destiny. No more sex between*
*us. Im fine! LULU.*

*Take off 2 set and cover the truth.*
*DO NOT MAKE ME EVIL. lulu*

I feared for her sanity. More often now I turned her away when she came…once I even threw her out in the middle of the night. ('You great, man, really great: LULU HOMELESS. LULU SLEEP ON STAIRS.') Once she came to my door at 6 a.m. dragging all her possessions in a suitcase on wheels behind her. She lost all control when I wouldn't let her in, pumping on the neighbours' door bells and screaming at the top of her voice. 'HE GOT OTHER WOMEN IN THERE!' 'Lulu,' I said, 'what if I have? What's it to do with you?' Her eyes narrowed and she came up close to me, her rage disguised by a soft, placatory smile. 'Because if Lulu find you with other women,' she said, 'LULU KILL YOU.'

I had decided, after years of resisting, to visit the cradle of modern culture, Memphis Tennessee – birthplace of the blues and rock 'n' roll, of Robert Johnson, Elvis, Howlin' Wolf, Chuck Berry. I was astonished by Memphis, by the glare of the lights and the blare of music on every street corner, by the character stamped on the faces of each and every one of its inhabitants. There was no-one in Memphis, it seemed, except they lived right on the edge of possibility. Every one in Memphis had a song to sing or a story to tell. Even the street beggars would sing you a song or perform a tap dance before asking you for money. I spent three months in Memphis living in a shack by a lake on the edge of town. When I needed to, I travelled into the city by bus – there were buskers on the buses, and everyone you met said 'Hi y'all' or 'Where you travellin' to, friend, where you been?' Everyone in Memphis wanted to know everything about you. It was like no other place on earth. I experienced a sort of spiritual homecoming.

On the plane back I was sleeping as we flew over the heartlands of America and then I awoke with a start. Suddenly everything fell into place, everything made sense. I had found my home, why couldn't this be Lulu's home too? Couldn't this be the place, rather than crumbling, seedy London, where Lulu could find herself? Where she would no longer need to retreat into madness or solitude? I imagined it as though it were real: Lulu and I living on Beal Street, going out every night to listen to the blues, coming back and making love until morning...then getting up early, going out to the early-morning cafés and coffee shops, and coming back with coffee-grounds and black-eyed beans and fresh catfish for breakfast. I would write my stories, she would paint her pictures. And music everywhere. I realised what I had been missing all these years, trapped in London with only my explorations for escape. My exploring days, it seemed to me, were over.

But I never saw Lulu again. I came back to London but this time there was no click clack click clack of heels, no text messages, nothing. I tried calling her but her phone was cut-off. I went round to her lodging house but the place had become a building site. I stayed in, I waited, but Lulu never came.

# The Bailiff's Story

I set off along the heat-glazed pavement down to the shady woods at the end of the road. I run through the woods, past the railway line and onto the common. I cut along a grassy stretch beside the lake, past the café where women and children gather after school. I run down to the bailiff's house.

When I reach the bailiff's house I knock on the door. After a moment or two the bailiff comes out.

'Yes, can I help you?'

I observe him coolly. Like most bailiffs he dresses as a woman: a tiny top, that clings to his falsies like cling film to ripe watermelons, a short frilly miniskirt, purple lipstick, high heels.

'Can I help you?'

'Are you the bailiff?'

'Yes.'

'There are some boys fishing by the lake. It's out of season.'

'What sort of boys?'

'Polish boys.'

'Hmm.'

'Shouldn't you take action?'

The bailiff shrugs. He has a thick pockmarked face and a bald head upon which is perched an elaborate auburn wig.

'You are the bailiff?'

'Yes, but I'm having my tea.'

I glance around. The house seems empty though there is a tray placed upon a low table in the sitting room and what seems to be the flickering of a TV set behind a glass panel.

'What are you watching?'

'Whose Life Is It Anyway.'

'And?'

The bailiff shrugged.

'I don't know. Could be anyone's.'

'But not yours.'

'No,' said the bailiff. 'Not mine.'

'Well, I thought you'd like to know. Kids. Kids from elsewhere. Polish kids. Eating the bloody coarse fish in the lake. Like they were starving or something.'

'I'll look into it.'

These bailiffs are all the same. They take the job, take the money, then dress up as women and watch TV all day. I run round the common and back, past the sparrowhawks' nest where the young hawks are stretching their wings in preparation for flight, to the flat where my son lives. There is nothing more important than family. Family is all we have. We are part of family not separate and entire whatever we may think. We may want union with God but we get union with family.

I shower beneath the electric shower, feeling better for the run. I do not run fast, little more than walking pace these days, but feel invigorated after each run nonetheless. I sit down with wet hair in the front room and my son and I play a few games of chess. As usual he wins, though he allows me to win the last one. I rise and shake him by the hand.

'Well played.'

'Thank you.'

'You are in charge.'

'O?'

'Yes,' I say. 'You are in charge.'

A smile creeps across his face.

'But watch out for the bailiffs. There is a bailiff down there dressed as a woman.'

'Okay.'

I get in my car and drive. I feel the sky travelling above me at the speed of light ensconced within the humming purr of the machine as I shift gears and speed out onto the motorway.

# The Illegitimate Boy

The illegitimate boy wouldn't look me in the eye, just stared at the floor and mumbled when I tried to speak to him. 'What's your name?' I asked him. Mumble mumble. 'For God's sake,' I said. He looked up, embarrassed and tongue-tied.

'You don't have to be frightened of me.'

'Not frightened of you.'

'Well you look it. Whenever I speak to you all you ever do is look at the floor and mumble.'

'Don't.'

'You do. You can barely string a coherent sentence together.'

'Can.'

'You want to go pick apples?'

This put the illegitimate boy in a state of confusion – he had no idea whether or not he was allowed to pick apples or whether I possessed the authority to invite him. He was kept hidden from the world. He was 'inferior' by virtue of his illegitimacy. It was understandable that he might not want to be my friend because being my friend might expose him. People might ask him, 'What does your dad do?' and he would say, 'I don't have a dad'. 'Don't have a dad?' 'No.' How come?' 'Because someone shagged my mum outside of wedlock and pissed off.'

He was only ten or eleven, too young to understand.

'No.'

'Why not? What's wrong with picking apples?'

'Don't know.'

'You don't know what's wrong with picking apples or you don't know whether you want to pick apples?'

'Don't.'

'Don't what?'

'Can't.'

'Why not?'

'Don't know.'

All this time the illegitimate boy was looking down at his feet and blushing.

'Look,' I said, 'I can see you're a shy kid. But it doesn't matter. I'm allowed to pick apples. You're my friend. So you can come pick apples too, if you want.'

'Yeah?'

'Yeah. And you can get to keep some. Maybe your mum will make you apple pudding.'

The idea of apple pudding seemed to resonate. He hadn't, I guessed, related apple picking to pudding eating.

Now this was clarified I could see an inchoate desire in the kid.

'Maybe.'

'Maybe you will or maybe you won't?'

'Not sure.'

'You want to ask your mum, is that it?'

'No.'

'So what?'

'Don't know.'

'Well come or don't come,' I said. 'We can't stand here talking all day. What do you do all day anyway, hidden away in the kitchen?'

'Puzzles.'

'Puzzles?'

'Yes.'

'What sort of puzzles?'

'Jigsaw puzzles.'

'You do jigsaw puzzles all day? That's no life. You should be out picking apples or riding a bike or painting chair-legs.'

'Maybe.'

'So, you want to come to pick apples or not?'

'Maybe.'

'Trouble with you,' I told him, 'is you can't string a coherent sentence together. You mumble like a simpleton.'

It was the wrong thing to say. The boy blushed and became unable to speak at all. Being accused of being a simpleton was too close to what he thought of as the truth. I didn't think he was a simpleton, just a kid fucked up by his circumstances. But he sometimes seemed pretty simple.

He mumbled and shuffled and blushed.

Then he lifted his eyes to my face and said,

'Not.'

'Not what?'

'What you said.'

'Okay.'

'Everyone says I am but I'm not.'

It was the longest speech he'd ever made, to me anyway.

I took him round the greenhouse and showed him the dead mice. 'Mice come out at night,' I explained. 'They come out looking for food and get caught in the traps. Bang, just like that.'

The illegitimate boy picked up one of the dead mice and stroked it.

'It won't come back to life,' I said.

We went up the garden to pick apples. Except the apples weren't ready and after we'd picked one or two we decided to leave it for another day. He was a funny kid though…kept finding bits and pieces on the ground and putting them in his pocket. Little odd-shaped stones and flints. Like he was an archaeologist or something.

'What are those for?'

'Dunno.'

'Well, why'd you pick them up?'

'Dunno.'

'You picked them up for no reason?'

'Maybe.'

We went to the very top of the garden and looked over the fence at the field that belonged to the people with the helicopter. There were two black horses in the helicopter field.

'I've never seen them before. Have you?'

'No.'

'You ever even been up here before?'

'No.'

'Do you like it up here?'

'It's okay.'

'You don't say much do you?'

'Sometimes.'

'Surprise me.'

He fell silent.

We looked in at my grandfather's hut and there was my grandfather sitting on an upturned log with a cup of tea beside him. He was sharpening an axe. He propped the axe up against the wall and greeted us.

'Come in, come in,' he said. 'Come and join me. I'm having a cup of tea. Who's this?'

'This,' I said, 'is the boy who lives in the kitchen. Perkin Warbeck.'

'I didn't realise we had a boy living in the kitchen.'

'There's a lot you don't realise Grandpa.'

'Not a boy living in the kitchen.'

'Well, this one is.'

My grandfather looked at the boy.

'You okay son?'

'Yes.'

'You don't look okay.'

The boy swallowed and blushed.

'Am okay.'

'You don't look okay. You look ill.'

But my grandfather had a kind side as well as a brusque side. He stroked the boy's cheek and murmured to him, something about the iniquities of the world and how with God's help you could overcome them. The boy looked up at him and smiled.

Then he changed tack.

'Well,' he said. He waved his arms about. 'We've got everything here. Beans. Raspberries. You like raspberries?'

'Don't know,' said the boy.

'Don't know if you like raspberries?'

'No.'

It was on the tip of my tongue to say, 'No use asking him, he's simple,' but I kept my mouth shut. Things were hard enough for the illegitimate boy without me making them worse.

# The Unnameable Fish

I walk down to the bridge to watch the swans. The summer teems with insects and the air is filled with martins, swifts and swallows. Blue and turquoise dragonflies skitter above the water, alighting on any protruding stone or branch before darting for their prey. The water is radiant with the reflection of their translucent, humming wings. The tall trees beside the river, decked in their summer foliage, are filled with flycatchers and warblers flittering and darting. I watch as a willow warbler flies out to take a Red Admiral; it eyes me, the intruder, the insect half crushed in its beak but still struggling, then dances away, bouncing over the bridge like a series of musical notes before disappearing into the trees on the other side of the river. The river is filled with boats too, navigated around gumbooted fishermen, the air filled with the shouts and cries of day-trippers as they are steer inexpertly across rapids and in and out of sudden eddies, spinning violently round or turning over to deposit their human cargo in the shallow water. They shout to each other, these day-trippers, boat to boat, or simply for the sake of shouting but their cries, unlike the birdsong, are for the most part unlovely. It is as though the sky and the earth and the water are invaded with alien creatures.

Above, so high they cannot be seen without binoculars, a red kite and a buzzard circle, the kite above the buzzard, circling in ever widening circles until the kite is directly above my head, high on the hot summer thermals, its colours clearly visible, its red forked tail turning gracefully as it glides and soars, its wings outstretched like enfolding arms, its neck craned down the better to see its prey.

The swan with her cygnets has moved downstream, out of the way of this commotion. I haven't seen her for three days. There are stretches on the river where the trees and brambles are so thickly entwined it is impossible to see, or hack one's way, through them to the river. It is in one of these stretches she hides. Now, there are just two swans left, a male and female, but without nest or young; they swim all day keeping a certain distance between them, their heads and necks vanished beneath the water leaving only their shoulders and their great white wings visible, or clamber, one after the other, onto one of the rocky islets that have appeared from nowhere and stand, cleaning their feathers, resting. I am about to lift my binoculars to watch them when Father Roger, accompanied by his acolyte, the shaven-headed poet from Oxford, comes on the path leading up from the bridge to the road.

I lift my hand in greeting.

'I don't see you for weeks and then we meet twice in two days,' he says, clambering up the path towards me.

'I'm beginning to agree with you about the heat.'

'The sun's friends are out in force again!'

He is wearing a black shirt, dog collar, black cassock. He has a giant poodle by his side.

He stops to pluck the fennel that is growing wild at the side of the bridge.

'I thought I spied a flycatcher here yesterday.' I wave my hand towards the stone wall that abuts the half-ruined house that backs towards the river.

'What's that, a bird?' says Roger, plucking fennel.

'They fly to and from the same perch. They catch insects then take them back to eat them.'

He sticks a piece of fennel in the pocket of my shirt.

'Here, have some fennel. It's perfect. We're having fish for dinner.'

'O. What sort of fish?'

'I don't know. I'm not the one cooking it.'

The Oxford poet is standing silent and sweating by his side.

143

'How are you? Hot enough?' I ask him.

'I don't mind the heat,' he murmurs, his eyes cast down. 'My room is nice and cool.'

He has come to make his peace with the world, this seeker of fishes. Rarely to be seen more than a few feet from Roger's side. It would not be a surprise to find him scourging himself with a whip. Is it he, I wonder, who will cook the unnameable fish?

Father Roger has a thick clump of fennel in his hand. He holds it up so only the thick, bushy part can be seen, above his coiled fist.

'It's like the Green Man's pubic hair!'

'How can you tell?'

He laughs his soft, melodious laugh.

'The world is full of danger and despair. And hope for the blessed. I have nailed the rood cross to the tree.' He chuckles again. 'That sounds like something out of a porno mag.'

The poet, sweating profusely, is anxious to be off. I heard him read once, at St Mary's Church, Capel-y-Fyn. He spoke of meeting Jesus on one of his riverside walks; but, he went on, he wouldn't know what to say to him. Jesus too would be rendered speechless. The two of them passing by like repelling like like a pair of tramps. One might try to sell the other a watch, purloined from some other passer-by, or consign the other's soul to purgatory.

I watch them walk away: two men, one tall and dressed like a woman, the other with his shaven head cast down, the poodle, jaunty and dainty, stepping gracefully between them.

# Crossing the Bridge

I was trying to impress a girl. She'd been riding pillion all day, apart from a couple of stops at service stations on the motorway.

The day had started off sunny but now was cold. I'd weaved through the traffic on the motorway at speeds of up to 150. We reached London and drove through the blackened streets averaging eighty, maybe ninety. The streets were empty and the lights had gone out. From time to time we heard singing, a strange haunting singing like the singing of someone in distress, someone who was about to die. The singing seemed to come from the air – not from the ground or the sky but somewhere in between. As though there were angels singing and they were singing a lament not a love song.

She was shouting in my ear for me to stop. I went down gliding and brought the bike in at the side of Farringdon Road. I remembered Farringdon Road from the old days when it served Smithfield Market, when there were book barrows lining the sides of the road, when people still read books. All those years ago. She slung her leg over the side of the bike, climbed down and stood by the side of the road in her leathers. She took out a pack of cigarettes, lit two, handed one to me.

'It's good to be here.'

'I know.'

'The past doesn't matter. All that matters is that we're together.'

'I know.'

She kissed me, twining her leg around mine, pressing herself to me. I dropped my cigarette and slid my hands inside her leathers, felt the soft skin of her back. Her skin was softer than anything I'd ever known, warm and soft as new-born skin. My hand was sliding across her back and she was kissing me, twined round me, pulling me onto her.

'Better not.'

'Why not?'

'We've got to get back.'

'There may be nothing there.'

'There may be.'

I ground out the dying cigarette with my boot, took another, lit it. We stood smoking looking at each other by the side of the road. She was smiling, happy. I was too tired to smile.

We climbed back onto the bike, I felt her arms slide round my waist, felt her head on my shoulder. 'I love you,' she whispered. I revved up the bike, glanced back to see the road was clear, slid out from the side, accelerated away. Down Farringdon Road, through the lights – red or green it made no difference now. We could hear the angels singing as we roared past Holborn Bridge, raced up towards Aldgate station. There was a figure of an angel on top of the station with his hands lifted to the sky. He was saying *i am cold and tired and ready to die*. I had heard that song a million times. I flattened the bike and straightened her up as we came onto the bridge. We must have been doing a hundred. As we straightened onto the bridge someone stepped into the road. I felt her shudder then her hands slid over me like an embrace and she was gone. I was trying to hold the bike but the bike was weaving out of control. It seemed to fall and slide into the side of the bridge and as it hit the side of bridge I too was carried up into the sky and flying. I looked down but all I could see was the bike split in two, one half rocketing across the bridge, the other embedded in the stanchion, smoke rising from the twisted blackened metal.

I was flying across the blackness, could see lights and stars in a single revolving motion like a kaleidoscope or a dream. Then I hit the water. I went into the water and found myself struggling up towards the light. I was being pulled down by my leathers and my boots were filled with water. As hard as I swam I couldn't seem to reach the light. My lungs were bursting with the effort of staying alive. I hit the surface and sucked in some air. The water was near freezing. I went under again, dragged down by my leathers. I was trying to remember the last things I'd said to her. I couldn't remember. Did I tell her I loved her? I was trying to unzip my leathers but my hands were freezing. My body was trembling and the strength was draining from me. I knew I had to get my leathers off or they would drag me under. I was fumbling with the zip, sinking beneath the water and forcing myself up again, gasping and choking. I had to reach the shore; if I could reach the shore I would at least survive. My zip was caught and I couldn't free it. I was tearing at my leathers trying to get them off trying to slide upwards out of them. Trying to kick off my boots in the freezing water.

She was swimming beside me. She said,

'I'll carry you.'

'How can you carry me?'

'I'll carry you on the wings of love.'

'You're not real.'

'I am real. I was your last pillion. Don't you remember?'

'I don't remember anything.'

'If you can't remember you can't live.'

'What does that mean?'

'It means you are your memories...'

She was floating away from me now. Smiling, reaching out towards me. I was trying to reach her. My leathers were off and I was floating naked in the water. I was a child again, laughing like a child – thinking, there is no-one to find me, no-one to see me, no-one to miss me. There were lights on the banks on both sides of the river but the two sides were equidistant and it made no sense to swim to one rather than the other. There were people on the bank waving and shouting, urging me to swim. But it was too cold then too warm. The colours were gone and the river and the city were monochrome.

# House of Imaginary Women

I knocked on the door and a woman answered – not the woman in question, no, but her maid. She stood quietly aside to let me in (sometimes they were old hags, over-keen to gabble, though not this one). She showed me to a chair beside a vinyl-covered table in the kitchen. I sat down. Another sat behind a discreet curtain in a cubby hole beside the hall. The maid was engaged in tea-making. Beside my elbow were copies of men's magazines.

'Isn't it awful, just awful?' she said, after a while.

I didn't know what she meant – that women like her and her charge had been reduced to this? That I, an otherwise perfectly adequate young man, had been driven to this place? – but no, it was the weather, I surmised, chilly for the time of year, and damp, to which she referred.

'Still,' I said, 'all good things must come to an end.'

The maid eyed me with suspicion.

I meant the weather. 'Isn't it awful?'

'It often is.'

'But so damp, for the time of year!'

She was making tea and I wondered if she would offer me a cup. I guessed not. No time for tea. The woman in question, engaged within her boudoir, was silent as the grave (how often these things are conducted in a perfect silence). Perfect silence and we would carry on, discussing the weather or topical triviali-ties, as though nothing were happening nor about to happen, until all at once there would be the sound of voices, male and female, the male deep and gruff the female light as a feather, a door open-ing, a farewell, a door closing. Then she, the woman in question, would appear at the door or the curtain of my hiding place and regard me. Look me up and down as a farmer might inspect a horse. 'In we go,' she would say, then, the one leading the other, to stand face to face in silence. 'Well?' she might say. We would discuss terms (so much for this, so much extra for that, this she would do, this she wouldn't, a variety like a variety of finches – though no sane woman would ever perform the same act twice).

'It isn't, actually. It's just that we haven't had much recently, but now this, all of a sudden.'

'And this!' she cried, picking up an early edition of the Evening News. 'What do you make of this?'

It was a headline about the Duke of Edinburgh and Lord 'Dickie' Mountbatten being involved in a plot to overthrow the Wilson government.

'We are living through interesting times.'

'Get rid of the lot of them, I say,' she said. 'They're as bad as each other.'

It was a neutral remark, as neutral as can be, at least insofar as it could be taken to mean almost anything (though not perhaps that she approved of the government).

'Do you pay much in tax?'

'Tax?'

She looked at me, one hand on the kettle, poised to lift and pour the steaming water into her tea-pot. I wasn't sure, at first whether she had heard me correctly – or perhaps she had but didn't know what tax was. Then it occurred to me that it probably wasn't the sort of question she was used to hearing, being preoccupied, as she was, with other matters.

'Tax? Don't we all darling!'

'Well we,' I said, 'you and I, we are their paymasters.'

'Now there's a thought,' she said, laughing.

'We employ them to do our bidding. Comme ci comme ca. That's what they're for. We cut off one of their heads once for refusing. Now here they are, still refusing.'

The woman threw back her head and laughed again.

'Yes,' she said. 'You can say that again.'

'Still refusing, as if we didn't exist.'

Then she seemed to forget all about me as she poured the steaming water carefully into the tea-pot and replaced the lid.

There was the sound, sudden and alarming, of a door opening close by and the sound of voices. A woman's voice saying 'See you later, darling', quite coarsely, and a man's voice returning in an undertone words I couldn't catch. The woman laughed and repeated her mantra as the voices and their accompanying footsteps headed towards the door. The door opened and, after another brief murmur of voices, closed.

'Rose?' said the maid.

'One moment darling,' said the voice.

There was the sound of a curtain being pulled back and then the voice again.

'Hello, darling. Come this way.'

The man, if it were a man, rose in silence and followed the woman along the passage to her boudoir. There was the sound of a door closing. The maid was poised over her tea-pot stirring the contents with a spoon, singing to herself in an undertone. 'Trouble trouble toil and strife.' I hadn't much cared for the sound of her mistress's voice, though I knew appearances (and sound is a sort of appearance) as deceptive: one of the most beautiful women I ever knew had a voice like a corncrake. Still, it had been more than a flaw in the cat's eye – it had somehow negated her, the sound of that voice in the throes of passion. Too loud and too coarse, like the voice of the hidden beauty in her boudoir. Still, the man who had accompanied her would stay or go. If he stayed I would leave. Time pressed hard upon me. If he went then I too would judge her, leave perhaps, my leaving no worse an offence than his. The maid continued to sing and stir, 'potage brew, how sweet you are, my love so true, just like a star,' while I waited. A heavy silence fell within which I saw the faces of my friends and family, imagining them witnessing me from some sort of static netherworld poised halfway between this world and the next. An old Frankie Vaughan song, something about 'variety being the spice of life', how there are 'as many ways to be as there are people to be them', floated into my head – a counterpoint to the witch's frenetic blatherings. I felt like raising my voice too in song and drowning out her misanthropic warble.

She turned as if reading my thoughts and pointed the spoon at me.

'They are all the same.'

'Who are?'

'All of them. Wilson, the Duke of Edinburgh, Mountbatten, King. All men.'

'They have to be. Men do…'

'Mind you, I'd rather have the Duke of Edinburgh. At least he's a gentleman.'

She returned to her stirrings and her warbling and I wondered if I had simply imagined this last exchange. Frankie Vaughan was dancing about in my head. He was wearing God knows what, a top hat and tails perhaps, and twirling a cane. He had a grin as wide and toothy as an aardvark. Like a frog in the window, bouncing up and down. Grinning so widely and toothily he seemed barely human.

Dreams. They swirl into your head then out again. But before they leave you manage to invest in them your entire future. Now I find myself at an open door – not one of those plastered with notices advertising Busty Blondes, New Young Redheads and so on – no, rather an anonymous door leading to an anonymous stairwell. Stairs leading up. Wide empty stairs with polished stair-rails and brown linoleum flooring. Up up up I go until I reach a long anonymous passage cased in the same brown flooring and walk the length of this passage and reach an unmarked door.

I knock and the door opens. There stands a girl – an anonymous girl, neither blonde nor busty, neither redheaded nor young, but a vague mixture of all these. A girl with no history, no name. She is eager to learn and eager to please, and I, in my dream, manage, before the dream flies, to teach her everything, every single thing, about me – but most of all about love. For love is an exercise of power, is it not. O, she is eager to please and pleases me alright. She wants nothing but my happiness.

And there is another dream, another establishment, an establishment on the east side of the city, a house filled with women, every one exceptional, every one available. Some are French, some Irish, some Arabian. They perform every act imaginable, and some that aren't; they know how to please beyond command, or rather that the command is implicit within the other's exact presence. I awake from these dreams satisfied but it is only a matter of time before my footsteps spin in the sand and I am back again in my house of imaginary women.

There was the sound of the door opening and voices. At first, I am nonplussed. Have they already done the business, in double quick time? But no, they have not. The time was insufficient. They have failed to agree terms and the gentleman is leaving. The footsteps make their way to the door contained within silence. The door is slammed.

Rose enters but does not appear to see me. She is a tall brunette with excessive mammaries and a hard, almost masculine face – not my type at all. She is wearing almost nothing – a pair of panties round her too-wide hips and a flimsy, almost diaphanous negligee. She walks towards the maid and says,
    'I'm dying.'
    'Have a nice cup of tea, dearie.'
    Rose shivers.
    'That one,' she says. 'He was a piece of work.'
    'Have a nice cup of tea, Rose.'
    She notices me, sitting there quiet as a ghost, and smiles.
    'Hello, darling,' she says. 'Little Lord Fauntleroy. I didn't see you there.'

'O yes, Rose.'

'Well, darling, what can I do for you?'

The conversation is as awkward as the silence that follows. I have always been a gentleman, not just a connoisseur of love. Not for me to stand and slap Rose across the face, watch her recoil, watch the anger dart into her eyes and subside, consumed by greed.

I rise up awkwardly.

'Don't you like me darling?'

'I have to go,' I say. 'I have to be somewhere.'

She walks towards me, puts her hand on my shoulders, looks into my eyes.

'There's no hurry, baby. What's the hurry? We're all going to hurry ourselves to death if we don't watch out.' She was too close, too fragrant to ignore. The coarseness of her voice had fallen like a veil, her voice had dropped to a sweet soothing purr, even her features had softened. 'Why shouldn't we get along? We can get along. Can't we get along?' And I felt the taste of her blood-red lips on my lips, her flesh, like marinaded ox-flesh, making me whole.

# Acknowledgements

Special thanks to

Rebecca Camu, Charlotte Grieg
and Michael Wigan